T0197306

DEMONICA

DEMONICA

Mary Shockley

DEMONICA

Copyright © 2019 Mary Shockley.

All rights reserved. No part of this book may be used or reproduced by any means, graphic, electronic, or mechanical, including photocopying, recording, taping or by any information storage retrieval system without the written permission of the author except in the case of brief quotations embodied in critical articles and reviews.

iUniverse books may be ordered through booksellers or by contacting:

iUniverse
1663 Liberty Drive
Bloomington, IN 47403
www.iuniverse.com
1-800-Authors (1-800-288-4677)

Because of the dynamic nature of the Internet, any web addresses or links contained in this book may have changed since publication and may no longer be valid. The views expressed in this work are solely those of the author and do not necessarily reflect the views of the publisher, and the publisher hereby disclaims any responsibility for them.

Any people depicted in stock imagery provided by Getty Images are models, and such images are being used for illustrative purposes only. Certain stock imagery © Getty Images.

ISBN: 978-1-5320-7173-7 (sc)
ISBN: 978-1-5320-7174-4 (e)

Print information available on the last page.

iUniverse rev. date: 03/22/2019

The day started out like many others before. The 20-minute commute home from work over the pass was nothing new to Jamie. The fog was thick, but by no means un-drivable. She had driven in much worse. She was approaching a slight curve in the road when, suddenly, out of nowhere, a vehicle struck her, sending her car plummeting end over end off a 40-foot cliff. The other vehicle stopped briefly, before speeding away. As she lay there, her thoughts went to her family, a young 6 yr. old daughter, Sharise and her husband Charles. She knew she was dying. She would never get to see her daughter grow up. How could she let Charles know what happened and who did this? Although she didn't know the person, she saw the vehicle and the face of the person at the wheel. She was fading in and out of consciousness. What could she do to tell her family what happened? By the time the emergency crews got there, she was totally unconscious.

Charles, who was also on his way home from work, came across the accident just after the emergency crews arrived. They had barricades up and he was stopped just behind them. At first, he didn't know who was involved, but had a terrible sinking feeling in his gut. He then saw the car as it was being dragged up the hill. He recognized it immediately. He leapt from his vehicle and ran to the scene. He was stopped initially by a police officer before he could get to the ambulance. He told him it was his wife's car. The officer was trying to tell Charles he couldn't go by "I am sorry, but you can't go beyond…." He was interrupted by Lloyd, the police chief. "It's ok. Let him in." Lloyd was one of Charles' best friends. He wasn't sure how to tell him that Jamie was probably not going to make it. It was not a comfortable conversation to have for anyone, but their friendship and closeness made it especially difficult.

"What happened, Lloyd? How could this happen? I just talked to her about 10 minutes ago. Why?" Charles was, of course, frantic and distraught.

"I don't know yet. Until we complete the investigation, I really can't tell you anything for sure. What I do know, is that Jamie has a very weak pulse her breathing is very shallow. She is in very bad shape. They are doing everything they can, but…."

"But what? She has to be ok. Sharise…. Where is Sharise? Jamie was supposed to pick her up. Where is she Lloyd? Where's my daughter?"

"I don't know. She was not in the car. Maybe Jamie hadn't picked her up yet. You go with Jamie to the hospital in the ambulance, I will have one of the deputies pick up Sharise and take her and your car to you."

Lloyd put his arm on Charles' shoulder. Charles pulled away from him. "Lloyd, you better find out what happened here! I want to know who did this and why. And I want to know as soon as you do."

Charles climbed into the ambulance and grabbed the mangled hand of his beautiful wife. The doors to the ambulance closed and they headed to the hospital. About half way there, Jamie lost her life. Charles was hysterical. The EMTs continued to try to resuscitate, but were unsuccessful. She was pronounced dead at the hospital upon arrival. The officer showed up, little Sharise in tow. "Daddy? What's wrong? Where's Mommy?"

All Charles could do was cry, and hold his little girl close to him

The investigation continued, but to no avail. There were no witnesses and scant evidence. Lloyd was working at his desk when Charles arrived. "What have you found out Lloyd? Anything new? Please tell me you have something."

"Charles, these things can take months or even years to figure out. We may never know what happened. The only thing we have to go by…."

"I know Lloyd, the paint on the side of her car. You know, I was thinking, someone had to have called the accident in, what about them?"

Lloyd had answered this question a hundred times if he had answered it once. Charles' frustration was evident, but Lloyd had no news. He answered the question once more, "Charles, the call was anonymous, they said they came upon the accident after the fact and there was no one there when we got there. I have sent the paint for analysis and don't know any more than I did last week when you asked me. I will call you as soon as I know anything. I know how you feel man, but I..."

"How can you possibly know how I feel!!!??? Have you lost the woman you love!!?? Have you had to look your 6yr old daughter in the eye and tell her that her mother is NEVER coming home!!?? I don't think so!! You find out what happened! You figure it out and you get me some answers. NOW!!" Charles slammed the door as he left the office.

Lloyd did know how Charles felt. He never told anyone, and wasn't about to tell Charles now, but several years ago, he lost his wife and 5yr old daughter on their way home from a school play to a drunk driver. The only difference was that he didn't have a daughter left to have to tell that her mother wasn't coming home. That's why he left and came here. He couldn't go on in the town where they had met and got married. He couldn't go to the same restaurants they went to, or the parks where they watched their daughter play. He thought about that the day of Jamie's death and again every time that Charles came in for information.

There were witnesses to Lloyd's wife's accident and it still took almost a year to find the person responsible for their deaths. Now he had to try to find answers with no witnesses and very little evidence.

It's now been 3 months since Jamie's death. Charles felt so alone as he walked the very beach they met on. He remembered how she would get up and run along the beach every morning before sunrise. She was intent on keeping her body in excellent shape. She was so beautiful. Her hair was long and black with just a tinge of red. It flowed like silk from her head. Her skin was so soft. She made sure to wear just enough sunscreen to keep her from burning and drying her skin out while still allowing a perfect tan. Her eyes were the color of the sky. He remembers how they shone with love every time she looked at him or Sharise.

He remembered the first day they met. It was a day much like today. The sky was clear and blue. The warm ocean breeze gently blowing. The waves' calm rhythm repeating itself over and over. The seagulls calling from overhead. It was paradise, at least then. He was with his parents, he was only eight years old at the time and she was six. He watched as she ran along the beach, her hair even then, flowed with such beauty behind her as she ran. Every time the ocean would touch her feet, she would run squealing away from it, then go back and do it again. He approached her, nervously, and introduced himself. They went to the same school, but had never seen each other before that day. They were, from that point forward, inseparable. Even then, Charles knew they would spend the rest of their lives together.

He was deep in thought, remembering that day, when he looked up and saw her. So beautiful. Her hair, a shade of gold he had never seen before, flowing behind her like satin. Her perfectly tanned body glistened in the sunlight. As she walked by, their eyes met, she paused, the mist of the ocean waves crashing onto the shore behind her. She was incredible. Could this be real, or is it only a dream? He started toward her and she rushed away. What had he done? Maybe it was only a dream. Either way, he headed home.

As he arrived at his beach side home, he was thinking how empty it has been since his wife died, their daughter so young. Not sure what to do, he had sent Sharise to his mother's house. He needed a little time to himself. So many questions. Why was Jamie taken so early in life? Who was behind the wheel of the other vehicle? Why so much suffering? It had only been a few months, but it seemed like a lifetime. Was there really another vehicle or was his friend, Tony, right? Was Jamie struck by another vehicle in a parking lot or something and just drove off the road in the fog? He was so confused right now. Lloyd had nothing new, no witnesses, and no real evidence, nothing to help with the investigation. Where does someone start to help with an ongoing investigation without stepping on toes or interfering? Maybe someone without a personal attachment. Charles knows a lot of investigators, but who could he get without a personal attachment? Maybe he should call Tony? Maybe he knows someone?

He was startled by the doorbell. He wasn't expecting anyone. He looked through the peephole and saw her standing there. The woman from the beach, was he dreaming again? He opened the door.

"Hello" she said. Even her voice was beautiful. He hadn't been dreaming. She was real. He stood there for a moment just staring at her. "I said, 'hello'. Are you ok?"

"I…uh…oh...sorry. I just…"

"I saw you at the beach earlier, and I just couldn't help myself. I felt bad about running off without saying hello, so I followed you home. Can I come in?"

"Huh? Oh yeah sure, come on in. I... uh..."

"Thanks." She looked deep into his eyes as she walked by him through the doorway. "My name is Monica; I live about a half mile up the beach. I rent the house from these people...they're kinda strange…but it's a nice house. Nowhere near as nice as this one though," she said as she looked around the entry way. She picked up a family photo taken by a friend while they were on a Caribbean vacation. "What a beautiful family, is this your wife and daughter?"

"Yes." He said as he took the photo from her and set it carefully back down on the table.

Monica could see the pain in his eyes as he looked at the photo. "Are you ok?" she asked.

He paused for a moment choking back the tears, "Yeah, I just…never mind…I'm fine."

Monica pressed more, "Let me guess, she left you and took your daughter with her. Right?"

"Huh? No. My wife is dead. She died a few months ago in an accident. I sent my daughter to my mom's while I figure out what to do."

"Oh. Sorry, I didn't realize. I am so sorry. What happened?"

"I really don't want to talk about it. So…. why did you stop by?"

"Well, when I saw you earlier today, I was immediately attracted to you, and I think the feeling is maybe a little mutual? So, I thought I should follow you home, introduce myself, and find out. I know that I can be a little pushy and forward, but it usually serves me well."

Charles was a little surprised by her answer. He was attracted to her, but it was still a little too soon in his mind. "Listen, Monica was it?"

"Yes."

"Listen, Monica, I am attracted to you, but…"

"But it is still too soon. I get it. I do. You really loved her, didn't you?" she interrupted.

"I truly do. She's my whole life. I am still having a hard time getting used to the fact that she is not going to come walking through that door. We were supposed to grow old together, and now……well, I'm lost."

"Well, when you find yourself, let me know. I don't live very far away and maybe we will run into each other again…I hope so. Anyway, I guess I should go now." The fact that Charles said "do" instead of "did" told Monica she needed to give him some time. "By the way, I didn't get your name."

"Sorry, my name is Charles."

"Charles." She said. "I should have known. You look like a Charles. Anyway, see ya around Charles."

After she left, Charles walked down the hallway to the bedroom, the loneliest room in his house. A large oak bed is in the center of the room. Matching oak dressing table, end tables, armoire, she had to have it all. He remembered the day she picked it out. It was raining hard; they ran across the street after she saw it through the window. She wanted a closer look. They went into the store where she decided that this was the perfect set for them. It was just what she had always wanted. The intricate design and hand carved bed posts. The solid construction. This would last a life time. It was perfect. "I just wish it wasn't so expensive," she said as she looked at it. "Maybe someday."

It took several months for Charles to save enough to buy this $4000.00-bedroom set. He wasn't making as much as the "big boy" lawyers yet, but Jamie knew he would soon. They could afford some of the luxuries in life, but not real extravagance. He didn't want Jamie to know that he bought it; he wanted it to be a surprise. She was so thrilled when she came in and saw it. He made her cover her eyes and he led her into the bedroom. She was almost as excited as when he graduated from Harvard Law School.

He had refused to marry her until he was a "real" lawyer and could provide all the necessities of life, and a few of the luxuries. The wedding was beautiful. Her parents, Mom, a doctor, and Dad, a successful lawyer himself, spared nothing for their only daughter. The home, a gift from her Aunt

Helen, was attractive, although not as much so as some of the homes in the area, and it was paid for. He and Jamie were debt free. Then, the news of a lifetime, Jamie was pregnant. It was a difficult birth; the baby was breech and they had to take it by C-Section. Charles was scared to death. Then they handed him his daughter. "It's a girl." The nurse said as she handed the wrapped bundle of joy to him. She was so perfect, so beautiful. They had a little difficulty deciding on a name. Jamie wanted her named after her mother, Janis; Charles wanted her named after his mother, Sharon. So, they combined the two and came up with Sharise. She was the most perfect thing they had ever seen. Her shiny black hair, her piercing blue eyes, a perfect angel. They had never seen anything so incredible, or so small. Her hands so small, her tiny feet; how could she walk with such tiny feet. They soon learned that those tiny feet would quickly become big enough to walk and soon after, run. They had a difficult time keeping up with this very small person. Charles often wondered how someone that small could move so quickly.

As he remembered his wife, he couldn't help but think about their little girl. Daddy's little girl. She just turned six. Her mother is gone. He was lost. He remembered her saying she was afraid she would forget her mom. "Sharise, my little angel, as long as there is sunshine you could never forget her. You look so much like her. She is always with us, even if we can't see her with our eyes, we can see her with our hearts."

He always tried to comfort her. Soon after the funeral, he knew that she noticed the change in her daddy. He cried. Daddies don't cry. He remembered as he was sitting on the edge of the bed crying, how she cautiously crept up to him, wrapped her arms around his neck and said, "Daddy,

I miss Mommy too. It's ok to cry. I love you, Daddy." He felt a tear run down his cheek as he heard her words again. He broke down and started to cry again, only this time not even Sharise was there to comfort him. She has been away long enough. He decided to go get his little girl and bring her home.

His mother's house is only a few hours away. As he drove up, he saw Sharise playing in the front yard under the ever-watchful eye of Grandma. "Daddy!!" she squealed as he pulled in to the driveway. She ran beside the car all the way up the drive until he finally stopped. "I missed you, Daddy," she said as he reached to open the door.

"I missed you so much my little angel." He had just barely opened the door when she leapt into his lap and wrapped her arms around his neck as tight as she could. "Sharise, honey, I love you very much, but Daddy needs air."

"Sorry Daddy," she said and gave him the most beautiful smile he had ever seen. Her whole face lit up when he gave her the stuffed dog he had picked up for her on the way. It was as if they had been apart forever. Now that they were together again, Charles did not want this moment to ever end. He saw his mother coming up behind Sharise and smiled at her. Sharise looked over and saw her. "Grandma, look at the doggy Daddy brought me."

As Sharon walked up to the car, she saw the smile and she knew that he was truly going to be alright. He may not be over Jamie's death, but at least he was smiling. That was something she hadn't seen in months. "That is a real nice dog dear. Why don't you go show Grandpa? She patted Sharise on the head as the young angel headed in to show Grandpa her new "pet".

Charles could not help smiling seeing his family again. "Thanks for watching her for me Mom. I think I am ready to be a daddy again. I just needed a little time to think."

His mother looked at him in a way that only a mother can, with love, hope and understanding. "Charles, why don't you sell that big ol' house and come home. Sharise needs a mother figure around and I think Lloyd needs a break from you. I don't pretend to think that I could ever be her mother, and you know I will not interfere…"

"Mom, you and I both know you always interfere. That's what you do best." He said with a grin.

"Now, Charles, really. I would never interfere with the way you raise your daughter. It's just that…"

"I know, 'it's just that Mom knows best' right?"

"Oh, Charles, Please. I really just want to help. You have so much to deal with right now. Your father and I just want to help. It's hard to be a single parent, especially to a daughter. You have to worry about daycare after school and during the summer, a proper education, peer pressure, oh and dating of course. There will be things that come up that, quite frankly a man just can't deal with. Like her first bra, her first "cycle", and I don't mean "bi"-cycle, questions that you should not have to try to answer, and she should not have to ask her father. I know you. You don't like answering those kinds of questions. You don't talk about your feelings with her, and because of that she won't be able to talk to you about hers. It's not a bad thing; it's just the way you are. She needs someone to talk to about her feelings and the changes that are happening now and those that are still to come. Please, Charles, just think about it."

"Mom, you know that I love you. I don't want to burden you and Dad with our problems. We've got each other and we'll be just fine. Besides..." He said as he kissed her forehead, "you're only a phone call away right? And as far as Lloyd is concerned, he doesn't get a break until he finds out who murdered my wife."

"Murdered!? What do you mean murdered? I thought it was an accident. Did I miss something?"

"No. I just can't believe that she just drove off the road. She was a better driver than that. Besides, there was red paint on the side and back of the car. That tells me that someone ran her off the road."

Sharon shook her head, "She may have been hit in a parking lot you know. Just think about what I said, ok?"

"Alright mom, I will think about it."

Just then Sharise came running out of the house. "Daddy, Daddy, Grandpa said we could go out to a movie tonight if you say it's ok. Can we Daddy? Pleeeease?"

She had a way of looking at him that no father could possibly refuse. "Well, we'll have to see what's playing and...."

"It's this new cartoon, and I really want to see it, and Gramma and Grampa said we couldn't go until you came back and now your back."

Charles knew there was no winning this battle. "Alright, we'll go. Go get your sweater."

"YAY!! Grampa, he said yes! He said yes! He can't asist my charm." she squealed as she went back into the house. Charles found it very cute the way Sharise mispronounced words and had to smile.

Sharon beamed with delight. Such a charmer this little girl, and she knew it.

After the movie, Sharise, weary from the excitement of the day, filled to the top with movie theater popcorn and goodies from the snack bar, fell asleep long before they reached the driveway. Her father gently removed her seatbelt and carefully carried her inside. After gingerly placing her in bed, removing her shoes, and covering her up, he gently kissed her forehead and whispered "good night my angel" He tip-toed out of the room and turned out the light. He slowly walked downstairs. He, too, was exhausted from the day's events. He walked into the kitchen where his mom was making tea. "Would you like a cup of tea, Charles?" she asked as she began to pour herself a cup.

"No thanks, Mom. I just came in to thank you both again and to say good night."

"Good night, dear." his mom said as she kissed him on the cheek.

"Good night, son." his dad said without even looking up from his cup of coffee. Charles left the kitchen and headed up to bed.

His father Jack, is a man of few words. He rarely said anything that wasn't pried out of him. He was a very tall, handsome man. Clean cut and clean shaven. He really didn't like the look his son had acquired since Jamie's death. "A man should have short hair, and, if he has a beard, it should be neat."

Sharon reassured him, "As soon as he works through his current problems, he will return to being our clean-cut young man. He just has a few things to work out."

"He needs a shave and a haircut." Jack Sloan had said all he was going to say. He went upstairs and went to bed. After all that, Sharon was left alone with her cup of tea that she decided she didn't want after all. She turned out the light and went to bed.

The following morning was typical for the coast. The fog rolled in, the cool mist saturating everything. Sharise awoke early to beat her daddy downstairs. She went into the kitchen and under the watchful eye of her grandpa, who always got up before dawn, she pushed a chair up to the counter. Very carefully, she tip-toed over to the pantry; she didn't want to wake her daddy; she pulled out the box of Choco-puffs, her favorite cereal and carried it over to the counter. She went to the refrigerator, opened the door to get the milk out and everything in the door fell out onto the floor, startling her. She let out a scream. Of course, now, everyone was up. Her father ran into her room; his heart beating a mile a minute. He ran smack into his mother who was headed down stairs. She knew where the scream had come from, but now would be delayed getting there after being knocked down by her only son. By the time the two of them arrived in the kitchen, Grandpa Jack had already cleaned up most of the mess. "Stuff fell out and she got scared. Grandpa took care of it while you two were playing 'keystone cops' upstairs." Sharon and Charles started laughing with relief after they realized that everything was ok.

Sharise looked so innocent standing there, covered in milk from head to toe. "I was trying to surprise everyone with breakfast, see." She pointed to the table where there were four bowls of cereal, ready to eat. Jack had given her what was left of the milk so she could finish making breakfast.

"The bottles didn't break. Tops came off when they hit the floor." Jack explained as they all walked over to the dining room table.

"I see." Sharon said.

"A gourmet feast young lady." Charles said as he helped his young daughter into her chair.

"I hope that means you like it, Daddy."

She beamed with pride when he said, "It is the best-looking breakfast I have ever seen."

She looked at him and said "Better than Mommy's?"

Charles felt a lump in his throat and a silence came over the room. She was waiting for an answer. She knew she probably shouldn't have asked it, but it was too late to take it back. She missed her mother's breakfasts. Pancakes, eggs, sausages, bacon, the works. She just wanted to help fill in for her and show her daddy that she could help. She wanted someone to tell her she was doing a good job. It seemed like an eternity had passed. Charles finally looked up at her swallowed the lump in his throat and said, "It's very close Angel, very close." She was pleased. Her father had made her so proud of her breakfast. He was trying very hard to hide his pain. He tried to smile whenever Sharise looked up from her bowl. She knew he was faking.

Later that morning she climbed into his lap. "Daddy?"

"Yes Angel."

"I'm sorry I made you sad this morning. I didn't mean to. I was trying to make you happy. What did I do wrong?"

"Oh, my little precious angel. You didn't do anything wrong, I just really miss your mommy."

"I miss her too Daddy, but remember what you said, 'even if we can't see her with our eyes, we can see her with our hearts.' Remember Daddy?"

"I remember, Angel. It's just that I miss talking to her and having her next to me."

Sharise looked at him with an understanding gaze beyond her six years. "Just do what I do Daddy. Look at a picture of her and start talking." She pulled his ear down to her level and whispered, "But you better do it when you're by yourself or people might think you're crazy." How could he resist smiling at that? She wasn't sure what she had done, but her daddy was smiling, and that was good. They hugged as if there were no tomorrow. Sharon was standing just on the other side of the door and overheard this conversation. She smiled. She was glad that Charles had listened to what she had told him concerning talking to Sharise about his feelings. She still hoped that he would change his mind and stay home, but this at least was a step in the right direction.

That evening, Sharon decided that Charles and Sharise should go somewhere, anywhere, just to get out of the house. She felt they needed some time together, just the two of them. She suggested they go to the carnival. It was in town for a few days. Sharise of course thought it was a great idea. As they walked through the midway, Sharise could not contain her excitement. She wanted to play every game and ride every ride. "Please Daddy, just one time." She said at everyone. They rode as many rides as time, and her age, would allow. As they were waiting in line to get cotton candy, Charles heard a familiar voice. "Charles? Hello again. I didn't expect to see you here. Is this your daughter? She is more beautiful than her picture." It was Monica. He was pleased to see her, although Sharise, most visibly, was not.

Right away Sharise felt that something was wrong with this woman. She had never seen her before, but there was something about her, something strange. She noticed the way her father looked at her. It was a lot like the way he looked at her mother. She knew this woman was going to be trouble.

"Hi Monica. Yes, this is my daughter Sharise. Sharise, this is Monica. Say hello." Charles was hoping that they would hit it off right away. He really liked Monica. Something about her intrigued him and made him feel like they were meant to be together.

"But Daddy, you told me never to talk to strangers." She looked at Monica with daggers in her eyes. She didn't like her and didn't care if she knew it or not.

"Sharise, honey, Daddy knows this lady and it is ok to say hello to her. She's not a stranger anymore. Don't be rude."

"I don't know her. That means she's still a stranger to me and I can't talk to her." She said very matter-of-factly.

Charles was beginning to lose his patience with his little angel, "Honey, I just introduced you to her, that means she is not a stranger anymore and it is ok to at least say 'hello' let's not forget our manners."

"Fine. Hello lady." She said it as if she were spitting at her. "Happy now, Daddy?" The daggers in her eyes told Charles that not only did she dislike Monica; she did not like being forced to do something she thought was wrong.

"Sharise!" he snapped. Then he looked at Monica, "I'm sorry, I really don't know what to say. She is still having some trouble with the loss of her mother."

Monica knelt to the little girl's level, trying to get some kind of acceptance from her. "I'm sorry you lost your mommy, honey. Maybe you just need someone to talk to about it. I'd like to help you if you will let me."

Sharise glared at her as if she were trying to burn a hole right through her. "I don't think so. I talk to my mommy all the time and my daddy too. I don't need you or want your help. I don't like you."

"Sharise!!" Charles couldn't believe what he was hearing. "You shouldn't talk that way to anyone, especially an adult. I taught you better than that. That was very rude."

Sharise gazed up at her father. "But Daddy, you always told me to tell the truth, no matter what."

Charles looked at Monica, "I am sorry; I don't know what to say."

"Don't worry about it. She's just going through a tough time right now. She'll be ok."

Charles decided to try to lighten things up a little. "So, what are you doing here anyway? Don't tell me, you rent a house just a little way up the road, right?" he chuckled.

"No, I have some friends that I came up to visit, that's all. I got bored sitting at the house, so I decided to get out and have some fun. They are great people, but a bit stuffy." She giggled. "I never even imagined that I would run into you. I'm glad I did though."

"I'm not." Sharise said under her breath, hoping her daddy didn't hear her, but pretty sure he did. Her father looked down at her with disapproving eyes. She knew he heard her.

"I don't think I am wanted here. I better go." She said as she looked down at the angry little girl. "Maybe I'll see ya around." She started to turn to leave.

"Wait. How do I get in touch with you? I mean…. I thought…. maybe…. we could…. I don't know; maybe get to know each other a little? Maybe have dinner sometime?"

She wasn't sure if she should answer with his daughter there. It was very apparent that she did not like daddy "getting to know" anyone yet. "My number is in the book. My last name is Moloch. Call me," she said as she winked at Charles. She knelt down to Sharise's level. "Good-bye Sharise. I'm sorry you don't like me. Maybe we can become friends later, huh?"

"Don't count on it lady." Sharise made sure that everyone heard that. She didn't like Monica and wasn't going to pretend that she did.

As Monica left, Sharise looked up at her father. She could see that he was very upset. "I don't understand you, young lady. I am *very* disappointed in you. Why were you so rude to her? She is really a nice person." She couldn't answer him; she was too upset. She never heard him talk to her like that before. She didn't know why she didn't like this new woman, just that she didn't. Tears rolled down her dainty little cheeks. She didn't want to upset her father, but she couldn't lie about her feelings. This woman wasn't as nice as her dad thought she was, and Sharise knew it. She was afraid this would cause her daddy not to love her any more. She was scared now, and the only thing she could do was cry. "Come on, Angel, don't cry, please. Look, Daddy loves you very much. I just don't understand why you acted the way you did. Come here." He said as he knelt down and held out his arms.

Sharise wrapped her little arms around his neck. "I'm sorry, Daddy. I love you too." She sobbed as she held him as tight as she could.

"Come on kiddo, let's go ride the Ferris wheel one more time before they close."

"But Daddy," she said as he wiped the tears from her eyes, "we haven't got our cotton candy yet. We can't leave without cotton candy."

"You're right. We'll get that first, and then go on the ride."

"Okay Daddy." He finished wiping the tears from her face, got back in line, and got the candy and a soda.

The Ferris wheel was Sharise's favorite ride. She said it made her feel like she was "flying over the whole wide world". Only this time was different. Her mommy wasn't there with her. They made it just in time for the last ride. She looked at her dad when the wheel stopped at the top, which was her favorite part, and said, "Daddy? Do you think Mommy can see me from here?"

"Yes, my angel, she can see you. She can see you." He looked down at his little girl and smiled. She smiled back and, before the ride was over, was fast asleep. It had been a long day, and it was very late. As the wheel came to its final stop, Charles nudged his sleeping angel to wake her. He was not successful. He picked her up very gently and carried her the three blocks home. His arms hurt by the time he got there, but it was well worth it when she looked up at him as he laid her in her bed. "Thanks for the ride Daddy; it was the best one of the whole night." She closed her eyes and was fast asleep again.

Sharise was still asleep when everyone else got up the next morning. As they all sat down at the table, Sharon could tell that her son was preoccupied. She wasn't sure if she should pry or wait for him to tell her what was on his mind. He just sat there, staring into his coffee cup. "So, Charles, would you like some flour and salt for your coffee?" She said trying to get him to respond.

"Sure, Mom," he said, without even looking up.

"How about some hot sauce and cream."

"That sounds good."

"Alright, son, what's wrong?"

"Huh?" Charles finally looked up from his coffee.

"I just asked you if you wanted flour, salt, hot sauce and cream for your coffee and you said 'sure'. So, unless you have some kind of weird new way of drinking coffee, I would say there is something on your mind. Would you like to talk about it?"

"I was just thinking…. what you said the other day about Sharise needing a mother figure…I think you're right."

"Really? Great! I am glad to hear that! You know I have a friend that sells real estate, you can list the house and…"

"No, Mom. That's not what I meant."

"Oh. Well, if you really want to just leave her here, we can take care of her for you. She will be here whenever you want to see her." She said, a little confused.

"No, mom. That's not what I meant either. I meant someone else."

"Son, if you think that you are going to put her up for adoption to be raised by a perfect stranger, then you and I are gonna have words, boy. That will just not happen. I…"

"What!? No. I would never even think about that. It's just…oh, never mind."

"I noticed that Sharise is sleeping in this morning. No early morning crash and scream." Sharon said with a smile, trying to change the subject.

"Yeah, we had a late night last night. We stayed at the carnival until it closed. She had a pretty good time, mostly."

"Mostly?"

"I kinda ran into a person."

"What do you mean 'ran into'? Do you mean you literally ran 'into' them or that you met someone that you didn't anticipate?"

"That's what I was trying to tell you. I met someone that I didn't anticipate…. a female someone. I don't think Sharise was very happy about it."

"I don't blame her."

"Mom…."

"What? It hasn't been that long since her mother died. What do you expect her to do? Just let someone else try to take her mom's place?"

"I just met this woman; she is not trying to take Jamie's place."

"Really? Yet you are talking to me about Sharise having a mother figure around. And you know this woman that well? You said you just met her? When? Where?"

"Oh, Mom. There you go making assumptions about people again. Can't you…"

"What? Can't I want you to remarry less than a year after your wife dies? No. I can't."

"Who's talking about marriage? I was just talking about…maybe…I don't know what I was talking about. Never mind, just forget it."

"Oh, so you start this conversation, and then just want to forget it happened. You started out by saying that I was right about Sharise needing a mother figure around and then tell me I am wrong about you talking about getting remarried. What am I supposed to think? I don't know what is going on in that head of yours, son." She turned to her husband, "Jack, do you hear what your son is saying? He's crazy."

Jack, without lifting his eyes just replied, "Uh-huh."

"Both of you men are nuts." She said as she picked up her cup and went to the coffee pot to get another cup.

Just then Sharise walked in, still a little groggy. "Mornin' Daddy. Mornin' Gramma and Grampa. What's for breakfast?"

"Morning Angel." Charles said as he got up from his chair. "It's almost lunch time. What would you like to eat?"

"Ummmmmm……pancakes."

"Ok, give me a minute and I will make you some."

"Like mommy's with chocolate chips?"

"Sure." Charles said with a smile.

"Charles, don't think this conversation is over young man. We will discuss this more later." His mother was not happy at all, and Charles knew it. He Wished he had never said anything.

After "brunch", Charles was sitting on the front porch with his dad, watching his little angel play in the front yard.

When his mom came out and sat next to him, he did not acknowledge her presence for a while. They just sat there watching Sharise play in the front yard for quite some time without saying a word, which was very unusual for her. She finally broke the silence, "Charles, I know you are lonesome, but don't you think it's a little too soon for that little girl to see you with another woman? It really hasn't been that long for either of you. I think you really need to think about this."

"I truly don't want to talk about it Mom." He said without even looking at her.

"I don't care! You need to talk to me. This little girl just wants to have someone that loves her and trusts her. You said she doesn't like this woman, what was her name?"

"Monica."

"So, your little girl doesn't like her. Maybe there is something to that. You know kids have a sixth sense about people. Don't you think you might want to listen to her?"

"Look, Mom, I know you're trying to help. But, please. I really don't want to talk about it."

"Fine. Don't. But I do. So, this is what I am going to say about it. You are hurting right now, and rightfully so. But, so is that little girl of ours. If you can't see that, then you don't deserve her. So, I have no choice but to keep her here." She said as she stood to go into the house.

"Stop, Mom. I am not leaving my daughter here. You and I both know that you are only saying that to push me into talking about this. So, ok, you win. I met Monica on the beach."

"The beach?"

"Yes. The same beach Jamie and I met on. She was walking down the beach, her hair shining in the sun. Then, she left. I went home. I was sitting there in the house when she rang the bell, I answered the door, she introduced herself, we talked and she left. Then when Sharise and I were at the carnival, we ran into her. She really wanted to reach out to her, but Sharise wanted nothing to do with her. I think she may be the one, mom. I really do. She's pretty and really a nice person." He finally turned to look at his mother, "I am not looking to replace Jamie. I have always loved her from the very day we met and always will, but she is not coming back, and I have to move on. I think it's what she would have wanted. I just wish my little angel would see what I see. I think they could become friends."

Sharon just shook her head, "Don't you think it is a little too soon though?"

"You keep saying that, mom. How long should I wait? It's not like my wife left me and we are waiting to see if she will come back. She's gone. All the way. I still miss her, but how long do I need to wait before I move forward instead of dwelling on the past? I need someone. Someone to talk to, someone to hold, someone to…."

"You know, that little girl is not someone to be ignored, son. How well can you possibly know this woman? You locked yourself up in your room for days after the funeral. Your father and I had to come up there and take care of both of you until we finally decided to just let you have your space and took her home with us. Now, you show up and tell us all that you have met this woman and want us to accept that she is 'the one'. Yet earlier you said you weren't talking about marriage. I don't know what to think. You said you just met her, but are trying to get your daughter to accept her already. How do you know she is not a criminal or something? Maybe she looks for lonely rich men and moves in to take them for all their worth. You need to slow down. If not for your sake, then for the sake of your daughter."

"Come on, mom, you make it sound like we are getting married tomorrow. I have only known her two days, but there is something about her, I feel …. connected to her."

"Two days! Only two days! Boy you really need to slow down. Check her out. You have the resources, find out about her. Do a background check. Something."

"I really don't think she is a criminal. She doesn't seem the type. Even when Sharise was rude to her, she understood. Not angry or even upset. She herself said that she just needed some time. She even told her that she hoped they would be friends someday." He said as he turned back to Sharise. "Does that sound like a criminal?"

"Even criminals want to have friends." She said as she looked over to her husband. "Jack. Why don't you talk to your son, help me out here?"

He did not answer her.

"Jack!?" she repeated.

"Coffee's cold, better get another cup." Jack said as he got up and walked back into the house.

"Such a help." She said with disgust. "Charles? Where are you going?"

"Sharise," Charles said,

"Yes Daddy?"

"Get your things together honey, we are going home."

"But, daddy, I don't want to go home yet. I am having fun."

"Charles," Sharon said as she grabbed his shoulder. He turned around to face her. "I'm sorry; I guess I'm just a little over protective of you both. So, tell me more about this woman you met."

"You really want to hear about her?"

"Yes. I guess if she brings out this much passion in you, she can't be ALL bad." She said as she sat down on the swing.

His face lit up as he started talking about her. "She's beautiful, mom. I can't explain it, but I can't stop thinking about her. Her name is Monica Moloch, kind of a strange name, but enchanting. She wants so much to get to know Sharise and be her friend. She really doesn't want to take over, just get to know her, you know. I can't explain it Mom, I just know that she is special."

"Hmph. How do you know that? You've only known her two days and spoken to her what... twice?"

"Mom, I really thought you were ready to listen. I guess as usual I was wrong. Sharise we are going home now. Get your stuff."

"But, Daddy"

"No 'buts'! Get your stuff together now!" He yelled.

Sharise ran, crying into the house to get her belongings. Her father had never yelled at her like that. She didn't know what to think.

"So, Charles? This is what this woman does to you? Comes into your life and makes you yell at your daughter and turn against your family? She's the one huh? You need to grow up boy." Sharon went into the house to help her little girl get her things and hopefully calm her down a bit.

Charles went upstairs to talk to his little girl. His mother was sitting on the bed holding his sobbing child. He looked at his mother and gestured for her to leave the room. She sat the heart broken little girl on the bed, got up, and reluctantly walked out of the room. Sharise laid there on the bed facing the wall, her sobbing continuing. She would not even look at her father. He had never yelled at her like that before, and she was hurt. She didn't even know what she did to make him yell. He wasn't sure what to say. He sat on the bed next to her and laid his hand on her back. She pulled away from him. "Angel?" He said as he pulled his hand back and dropped his head in shame. "I'm really sorry I yelled." She continued to look away from him, but the sobbing slowed a bit. "Please look at Daddy." She just laid there. He reached for her again; she got out of bed, stuffed puppy in hand, went into the bathroom and locked the door. She wanted nothing to do with him right now. She sat on the edge of the bathtub clutching the puppy with all her strength. She dropped her head into the shoulder of the animal and started sobbing into the soft fur of the only friend she felt she had left, other than Gramma and Grampa of course. Charles went to the door. "Honey, I really am sorry. I'm not angry with you. Your grandmother and I were just having a bit of a disagreement and…well…. I hate seeing you hurting. Please come out. I didn't mean to make you cry." He was leaning against the door when it opened. He almost fell into the bathroom. Sharise stood there with tears still running down her little face.

"Daddy, what did I do to make you not love me anymore?" She said with a pleading look in her eyes. "I just wanted to stay here for a while longer; I didn't mean to make you not love me."

Charles was taken aback with his little girl. He never wanted her to think he didn't love her. She was his whole world. Now he had hurt her and had to try to explain himself. "Sharise, my little angel, I will always love you" He said as he placed his arms around her. "You are my everything, my whole world."

"No matter what?" She asked.

"No matter what." Charles reassured her.

While he was calming Sharise, Charles' mother went into the kitchen where jack was getting another cup of coffee. "Jack, your son is impossible. There's no way he can expect that little angel to accept this woman so soon. She's not ready yet. He isn't either as a matter-of-fact. He's only known her two days. She's after his money, that's what it is. Well, she can have it." She said getting herself a cup of tea. "But she can't have my son or my granddaughter! I won't stand for it! He thinks he can just bring some strange woman into his home and expect Sharise to call her Mommy? I don't think so!" She was visibly upset, so much so that she didn't even notice jack left the room. He went back out onto the porch. She followed him, a little disgusted with him because he hadn't said a word. "Jack! I was talking to you. You weren't even listening to me, were you? You need to do something about your son. You need to stop him from making the biggest mistake of his life. Why are you ignoring me?"

Jack set down his coffee cup and looked up at Sharon. "I am ignoring you because you don't make sense. Leave him alone. You haven't even met her yet. Wait until you meet her, then, if she doesn't meet your standards you can get upset." He had said all he was going to, and Sharon knew it. She walked back into the house and into the kitchen.

She was sitting there when Charles and Sharise walked downstairs into the front room. Just as they reached the bottom of the stairs, Jack walked in. "Son." Is all he said when he walked by them. This was not unusual.

Jack turned and looked back at them. "Your mother is upset. She may not want to chat right now."

"Okay, Dad." Charles knew that was his dad's way of saying, 'don't make your mom any more upset or I will get involved.'

Charles and Sharise went into the kitchen to get a snack. Sharon was still sitting at the kitchen table when they walked in. "Charles, maybe I was a little quick to judge. If you like this woman, then maybe I should wait until I meet her to make any decisions as to whether or not I like her. I'm not making any promises, you understand, but I will put off my judgment until then."

Charles smiled, "Thank you, Mom. I didn't mean for any of this to upset you or Sharise," he said as he looked down on his daughter with loving eyes. "I promise I will not make any rash decisions about marriage," he said chuckling. Just then the doorbell rang. Jack was now upstairs so Sharon went to answer the door while Charles put the snacks together for him and his daughter.

"Hello?" He heard his mother say as she answered the door. Then another familiar voice "Hello is Charles here?"

"Yes, and you are…?"

"Monica. I just stopped by to see if he was going to be here for a while and…"

"And what? Find out when can you move in on him and his money?"

"Mom!!" Charles came running out into the front room. "I thought you were going to be nice and not jump to conclusions or judgments? I guess that was too much to ask huh?" He said as he glared at his mother with anger and disgust in his eyes. He then looked over at Monica. "Sorry, Monica. My mother is a little irritated right now. She is convinced that I am moving too fast. I tried to explain to her that we just met, and there are no plans for the future being made at this time." He glared back at his mother as she stood there, arms folded and obviously fuming. "Mom, can we talk please?" he said as he took his mother's arm and led her into the other room. "Look, Mom, I would really like for you to try to get to know her. You might even learn to like her. Please." He knew he was asking a lot of his mother.

"Alright, Charles. I will try."

"Good. Thank you. I will go get Sharise."

"Why? She is just fine where she is. She does not need to be exposed to her yet. I would like to talk to her alone."

"Um…. Ok…. are you sure?" Charles did not think this was such a great idea. "I mean…"

"What? You don't trust your mother to hold her tongue? You think I will say something you wouldn't like?" she said as she looked at her son with disparagement. "I promise I will keep a civil tongue in my head as long as she does the same. Trust me, son."

"Oh, I trust you Mom. I trust you to do whatever you feel is required to get your point across. I trust you to say what you think, when you think it regardless of anyone else's opinion. And, I also trust you to do the right thing when it comes to my life, and that is to do whatever you can to make me happy. Mom…" he said as he placed his hand on her shoulder, "what would make me happy right now, is for you to be nice to her."

He turned and went back into the kitchen. Sharise was sitting at the table staring at a plate of chocolate chip cookies. She hadn't even touched them. "Daddy?" She said without looking up from the plate, "are you and Gramma ok?"

Charles was a little puzzled. "Of course we are sweetheart. What would make you think we weren't?"

"You guys have never yelled like that before. I'm scared, Daddy, scared that you and Gramma are…"

"Don't be scared, angel. Sometimes adults get upset and yell. But your gramma and I are still ok. She's my mother and I will always love her."

"Ok, Daddy. You still wanna go home today?"

"Yes. We are still going home today. And please no more arguments. Ok?"

"Ok. Can I finish my cookies and milk first?" she said as she finally looked up from the plate at her dad.

"Of course you can." He said as he patted her on the head. He began to leave the kitchen when Sharise stopped him.

"Daddy? Why does gramma think you are going to marry that mean woman? You're not gonna are you?"

Charles stopped and looked back at her puzzled, "What makes you say she's mean? You only met her once."

"I don't know. She just is. You're not gonna marry her are you daddy? I don't like her."

"Why is everyone convinced I am trying to marry this woman!? I just met her myself. No. I am not planning on marrying her. Now eat your cookies." He turned and left the kitchen. Charles went up stairs and packed everything up. As he was carrying the suitcases down the stairs, his mother came around the corner. They walked into the family room together and saw Jack and Monica talking.

"Oh, Charles. You never told me you had such a charming father. We were just talking about your childhood. Jack was telling me what a wonderful, mischievous boy you were. I hope not much has changed." She said with a look of desire.

Sharon was less than impressed with her. She was trying to keep her promise to Charles and be nice to this person he was so convinced was "the one". "Would you like some coffee or tea?" She said through clenched teeth.

"No thank you Mrs. Sloan. I really must be going, I am headed home today and just wanted to stop and say goodbye to Charles and Sharise. I'm glad there still here. I was afraid I might miss them."

Sharon glared suspiciously at her. "Yes, well, that is something else I would like to know. How exactly did you find him here? How is it you know where I live?"

"That was easy," Monica answered; "I looked you up in the phone book." she looked at Sharon as if she were a total idiot. "Now Charles, where is that beautiful little girl of yours, I'd like to say goodbye to her too."

Charles couldn't take his eyes off her. "She's in the kitchen having a snack. I could go get her if you want."

Sharon spoke up, "You'll do no such thing, she earned her snack and I'll not have you interrupt it for this. She can just wait until she is done. Or maybe, just leave without saying goodbye. I am sure that Sharise will understand."

It was obvious to Sharon that this woman was pure evil. She would stop at nothing to get what she wants and what she seemed to want now is Charles.

She could not get past the distress that this woman has caused not only her, but, and most infuriatingly, her little precious Sharise. Now, knowing that Sharise doesn't like her, she wants to push the issue of saying goodbye to her.

"Your mother is right, Charles. Just say goodbye for me. I'll see her soon. When are you two leaving? Maybe I could stop by and we could have dinner or something." The only words that pleased Sharon were 'your mother is right.' "I would like to talk to Sharise. I don't think she understands. My intentions are not to take her mother's place but to be her friend."

"No, I think she understands your intentions better than you think. It's Charles I am worried about." Sharon said as she sent daggers with her eyes in Monica's direction. She then looked over at Charles.

"Mom? I thought you promised to check the attitude?"

"I tried, son, but I just can't do it. I don't like this one bit!" She stormed out of the room onto the front porch, sat down on the chair and stared into nothing. She could hear bits and pieces of the conversation, but not enough to make any sense of it. She did hear Charles offer to follow this woman home to make sure she got there 'safe and sound'. She began to get more and more upset until she finally could not stand it anymore. She got up to go inside and let these two inconsiderates have it when Charles came out.

"Mom, Sharise and I are going now." He said very calmly and matter-of-factly, "She just went to say goodbye to dad. She will be out shortly to say her goodbyes to you as well. I will call you later." He didn't even allow her to say goodbye as he walked down the steps of the porch and out to his car with Monica right behind him. Monica gave

Sharon a defiant, angry look. Sharon knew that if Charles had seen that, he would be a lot more accepting of her point of view, but was not going to bring it to his attention so as not to cause any more problems.

"Charles? Aren't *you* going to say your goodbyes to me?" She said while still looking angrily at Monica. "Or has this woman already taken your manners from you?"

Charles walked back to her and said, "Mom, Monica is the only woman here that has not made me feel like a child, or ridiculed me lately. And you have the nerve to talk like that about her? Then you talk to me about losing my manners? I will call you later."

"Son, don't think this is over. I will make you understand that this is wrong, and you and Sharise are better than her."

Charles, for the first time in his life, scowled at his mother. He went to Monica and opened her car door for her. "Sorry." He said as she got into the car. "I don't know what her problem is today."

"Charles, she's just protecting her little boy, that's what moms do. Don't be angry with her. She will come around sooner or later." Monica said as she started the car. "You'll see."

Sharise came out of the house and waited, patiently, for gramma to notice she was standing there. It took a little longer than she wanted, so she reached over and tugged on gramma's pant leg. Sharon looked down upon this sweet little girl that she just knew was being put in harms way, "Sorry, honey. I didn't see you come out." She knelt down and put her arms around Sharise. "I love you. And I want you to know, that no matter what happens I will always be here for you." Sharise was a little confused, she knew that her gramma and daddy were arguing, but now gramma sounds like she is upset about her and daddy leaving. Like there might be trouble.

As she was getting into the car she looked up at her father, "Why is *she* still here?" She asked pointing to Monica's car.

"We are going to follow her to make sure she gets home safe and sound. And we will all stop along the way for dinner at that restraunt you like so much. Is that okay with you." He said as he connected her seatbelt and went around to the driver's side of the car to get in.

"What!? I don't even like her and you're gonna make me eat with her!"

"Sharise, sweetheart, I think once you get to know her, you might like her. Just give her a chance, baby, please."

"I don't want to give her a chance, daddy. I don't like her and I never will. She scares me."

The conversation continued as they pulled out of the driveway. "She scares you? What do you mean she scares you? She's not scary."

"She is to me. I don't know why. I just…. I think she's mean…and she scares me…. she's like the devil."

"What makes you think that?" Charles asked as they headed down the highway. "What has she done to make you think she's like the devil? She has been nothing but nice to you. Even when you were rude to her, she was kind to you and understanding. She never once got upset. Even with what your grandmother said to and about her, she told me that your gramma was just trying to protect me and she understood. What about that makes her evil?"

"That's what I'm talkin' bout daddy, how many big people do you know would take that from a six-year-old? I don't know any. She's scary."

"Really? You think she's evil because she was nice to you! Look, we are going to dinner with her and that is final. And you will behave yourself like the angel you are. Ok?"

Sharise hung her head. She did not want to answer him. She was afraid that if she said ok, then forgot, that her daddy would get upset again. She didn't want that. Charles urged her for a reply, "Sharise?"

"I will try daddy, but if I forget, don't be too mad ok?"

"That, my dear, will depend on how much you forget."

Dinner went reasonably well. Sharise didn't say much, she was afraid that she would say something to upset her dad. After dinner, Monica and Charles exchanged phone numbers and, much to Sharise's disappointment, set another date. It was late when Charles and Sharise got home. She had fallen asleep long before they arrived. Charles woke her when he unfastened her seatbelt. He picked her up and carried her into the house, she had fallen back to sleep before they got to the door. He placed her gently in her bed and closed her door. He walked into the kitchen and poured himself a glass of wine. He then sat down in front of the fireplace and drank his wine and contemplated the events of the day. He was still confused about his feelings toward Monica, and his mothers and daughter's feelings against her. What could he possibly do to make them understand, she is really a nice person? She is not this evil being that they make her out to be.

Charles and Monica saw a lot of each other over the next few months. After about 5 months he proposed to her. She, of course, accepted. He wasn't quite sure how to break the news to his little angel. She still didn't like Monica and made sure everyone knew it. He thought maybe, if they went for a ride, she would take it better. At least then, she couldn't run up to her room and lock herself in until *after* he finished. She spent a lot up time up there lately. She refuses to come out even for dinner if *she* is there. The only way she will even listen to him when it comes to Monica is if they are in the car. He called to her. "Sharise,"

"Yes, daddy?"

"Would you come here please?"

"Is *she* there?"

"No, Monica went shopping. She wanted to take you with her, but I told her you and I were going to spend some time together today. I thought maybe we could go for a ride?"

Sharise wasn't sure about that. She knew he wanted to tell her something and if they were going for a ride, he was going to talk about *her*. She decided if she was going to have to talk about her, she was going to make the best of it. "Can we get ice cream?"

"Sure, why not. What kind do you want?" he asked as they walked out the door.

"Bubblegum with whip cream and chocolate sprinkles and…. bananas."

"Bananas, huh? And whip cream? Ok, whatever my angel wants."

She knew this was serious now. He never agreed to whip cream and bananas unless it was a special occasion. He said it would 'ruin her dinner' Now she was scared. He strapped her in, got in and started the car. "Seatbelt daddy." He had forgotten.

"Sorry, sugar. I forgot." He said as he pulled the belt across his chest and fastened it. "Thank you for reminding me." He pulled out and headed to the ice cream shop.

As they rode, Sharise was feeling more and more frightened about what he was going to say. "Daddy, whatcha want to talk to me about?"

"Who says I want to talk to you about anything? Maybe I just want to spend time with my favorite girl."

"Yeah, right. The only 'favorite girl' you want to spend time with is *her*. The only time we get together is when she's not here."

"That's not true."

"Really? Then you don't want to tell me something."

"Well…. actually"

"I knew it. And you tell me not to lie."

"I'm not lying."

"I want to go home now."

Charles stopped in front of the ice cream shop. He looked into the back seat where Sharise was. "Angel, daddy has some good news…"

"You're not going to see her anymore!!" she said with delight.

"Of course I am. You see…. Monica is going to be your new mommy. We're getting married. I want you to know that I will always love you as much as I always have, and that just because Monica is joining our family that doesn't mean that you and I can't be just as close as we have always been. You understand?"

"No. I don't want a new mommy. I just want my daddy back. I don't like her. She's mean to me when you're gone. She comes into my room and throws all my stuff on the floor and tells me I have to clean it up. She says if I don't, she will tell you I was bad and I'll get in trouble. She hates me. And I hate her too."

"Sharise...I think you're exaggerating. You know, making more of something than what really is. You think that you don't have to do what she tells you, no matter *what* it is. She wants so very much to be your friend. I can't believe that she would make you a slave or a 'Cinderella'. Please, try to get along with her. She's going to be living with us for a long time and I could never be without either of you. Please, try."

"NO! I won't! I don't want to call her mommy. She's not my mommy! I wish you would believe me! I'm not lying! She's mean to me! She hates me! And I hate her! I don't want you to marry her!!" she unfastened her seatbelt opened the door and got out of the car. She sat down on the sidewalk with her head in her hands and started to cry. Charles got out and sat beside her. He placed his hand around her shoulders. She pulled away from him.

"Baby, I know you don't like her. But she really does love you. She told me just last night how much she wished you would accept her. She loves you as much as she would her own daughter. I just want you to try to get along with her. She's really a very sweet person."

"No, she's not." She said between sobs.

"Sharise, honey, please. I love you so much and I don't like when you're this way. Just try."

"Do I have to?" she said as she lifted her head and looked at her father's pleading face.

"Yes. You do. I will always love you, but I don't like when you ignore her." He said as he tenderly wiped the tears from her face.

She still wasn't convinced that Monica was as sweet as her father thought, but she did not want to lose her daddy altogether. "Fine, I'll try. But don't spect too much. I'm not good at lying." Charles wrapped his arms around his little princess, picked her up, walked into the ice cream shop and ordered her favorite bubble gum ice cream with whip cream chocolate sprinkles and a banana and a large soda for him. Sharise started smiling and almost laughed when Charles blew the paper off the straw at her and hit her right between the eyes.

"You see, you can smile. And what a beautiful smile it is." Charles said as Sharise sat there eating her ice cream.

She looked up at him and simply answered, "I love you, daddy." They sat there for a while enjoying the ice cream and soda. The ride home was a little more tense since Sharise was now aware of the wedding, that she was definitely against. She knew her father will want her to be a part of it, but she is not sure she wants to be. *"Maybe I will get lucky and Monica won't want me in the wedding"* she thought. *"Maybe she hates me enough to send me away. No, daddy won't let that happen. He loves me too much to let her do that to me……. right? I don't know, he has been acting weird. Maybe he will let her do that…maybe he loves her more than he loves me. No. that's crazy. He loves me more. He would never let her send me away. 'cept maybe to grammas, and that would be ok."* by the time they got home she had convinced herself that there was no way that woman could possibly send her away. No way that her daddy would let her do that.

Charles had thoughts of his own…. *"What if Sharise never accepts Monica. How do I make her understand that Monica really does care about her? Maybe after the wedding, they will get along better. Monica will be around more and Sharise will see how much she really cares. She will come around."* They were both still deep in thought when they arrived at home. Monica's car was there. Charles was excited to see her. Of course, Sharise was not.

"So where did you two go?" She asked as Charles kissed her cheek. "I got home and you were gone. You didn't tell me you were going out. You just said that you were going to spend time together. You didn't even leave me a note."

Charles was a little confused, "I told you we would likely take a little ride. We went to get ice cream."

"Ice cream, huh? Did you get me some?" She asked as she looked down at Sharise.

"No, it doesn't exactly travel well." Charles snickered at the thought of Sharise holding ice cream for Monica.

"I see. So, did you have a good time? I sure did. I went to the mall and found some really nice clothes for the honey moon and then I got a manicure and pedicure. And you haven't even noticed my new hairdo. I just had to get it done again; it had been three days since I last went to the salon. I hope you like it." She said while walking away.

"I like it." Charles said.

"I don't." Sharise said under her breath. She hoped her daddy hadn't heard that, but by the look he gave her, he did.

Just prior to the wedding, Sharon tried to speak with Charles about Monica. "Son, I know you don't want my advice, but I spoke to the priest about Monica and he was very concerned."

"Oh, and why was that, mom? Did you tell him she was some kind of demon or something?"

"Actually, he made the conclusion."

"What!!?? What did you tell him mom? That she is pure evil? That she eats little children?"

"Of course not. Please listen to me Charles, I didn't even get past her last name. Do you know what it means?"

"Are you serious? I don't exactly look up last names of everyone I meet. And what even made you think about that? I mean who actually looks up peoples last names?"

"Charles, please. I didn't look it up until after I talked to the priest. I have to tell you…"

"What? What do you really HAVE to tell me? That her name means 'demon' or 'devil' or some kind of dragon queen? I really don't care what her name means. Do you know what our last name means? Honestly, if I was worried about everyone's last name and what it means, I probably wouldn't sleep at night."

"Once you find out what *I* did, you may *not* sleep at night. I know I won't. Her last name is a name given to a false god in the old testament."

"So now she is a god?"

"Apparently you are not familiar with this name, and neither was I, but I looked it up, and I printed it out so that you could see it because I knew you wouldn't believe me."

Sharon pulled out a piece of paper from her purse and handed it to him. He read what it said:

Moloch: [mōˌläk] in the old testament, a false god to whom children were sacrificed.

"This is ridiculous. I am not sacrificing my child to any god and you are out of your mind. Do you look up everyone's name or just those you think are devils? This doesn't change anything, I am still marrying her and there is nothing you can do about it. Now, you have said what you came to say, please go take care of the guests."

It was a beautiful wedding. Jack gave the bride away. Her own father had died several years ago. Sharise was the most beautiful flower girl her grandmother had ever seen. Of course, Sharon wasn't sure the bride should have been wearing white. After all that was reserved for purity, and Monica was definitely not pure as far as Sharon was concerned. She was not happy about this wedding. Especially since they have only known each other for a few months and his first wife passed away only 8 months ago. Then she thought to herself, "*oh, well, it's his life. I don't have to agree with what he does and, as long as Sharise doesn't get hurt in the process, I will not interfere.........much.*"

Jack didn't really have much of an opinion, he seldom expressed his opinions when he did have them. He felt that Charles' life is his own and the only way to learn in life was to make mistakes. If Charles is making a mistake it's not really his problem. After all, mistakes are the only thing you can really call your own.

After the reception was over and the guests went home, Sharise went into her room. She noticed that her bags were packed. She ran down the stairs, tears in her eyes and crying, "Daddy, why am I leaving!? She gets to stay!?" she said as she pointed angrily at Monica. "I thought I was s'posed to throw the flowers on the floor." She started sobbing uncontrollably.

"Honey, you are just going to stay with Grandma and Grandpa while we go on our honeymoon. Its only for a few days then we will be back."

"I want to go with you. You used to take me with you everywhere. How come *she* gets to go and *I* don't?"

Monica stepped in. "Sharise, a honeymoon is only for big people who are married, wittew giwls can't go. That's all there is to it." She said very smugly.

"I'm not a baby! Don't talk to me like that!"

Monica, realizing that Charles was within earshot, changed her tune quickly, "I'm sorry. You're right. Your father and I are going on a cruise and you can't go this time."

She paused for a moment, "I tell you what, we'll take you next time, ok?"

Sharise didn't answer her. She just stood there glaring at her.

"Sharise," Charles said, "your mother asked you a question. Please answer her."

Sharise stepped back stunned by her father's statement, then all she could feel was anger. "She is *not* my mother!!!! My mother is *dead!!* I wish *she* was too!!! I hate you Monica!!!!" she screamed as she ran to her room crying.

Charles yelled up to her "Sharise! You come back here and apologize to Monica. That was a very mean thing to say."

Monica placed her hand on Charles' shoulder, "It's alright Charles. She didn't mean it. She'll get used to me being around, just give her some time. She is just angry right now. She thinks you are trying to replace her mother. It's an understandable reaction. Just let her be alone for a while."

The drive to Sharon's house was uncomfortable, to say the least. Sharise stared out the window the whole way there and never said a word. Charles and Monica talked about the itinerary for the honeymoon.

They dropped Sharise off and Charles gave her a kiss on the forehead and a big hug. "I'll see you in a few days. I love you."

"I love you too daddy."

That night as she was lying in her bed at grammas house, she was trying very hard to figure out why her daddy didn't want her around on what some were saying was the happiest day since she was born. "Oh well," she thought, "maybe I will talk to gramma in the morning. She always helps me 'stand things." Then she slowly dozed off to sleep.

It was about 3:00 a.m. when Jack and Sharon were awakened by screams. "Mommy! Mommy! No don't go! I want my mommy!!!" They ran into her room.

"Sharise, honey, wake up, you're having another bad dream."

"Gramma, grampa, can I sleep with you tonight? I miss my mommy. I don't want to be 'lone."

"Of course you can sweetheart. Come on. Don't forget your pillow and your dog."

Later that morning, while Sharise was still asleep, Sharon and jack sat down to have their morning coffee. "Jack, I am worried about Sharise. These nightmares should have stopped by now. I am going to call Bill."

"A shrink? You think she really needs that. Hasn't she got enough to deal with?" Jack said not even looking up from his morning paper. He didn't really care for psychiatrists. He felt that family matters should stay in the family.

"Well, now, I think a psychiatrist may be just what she needs. She lost her mother, her father, your son, brings this bimbo into her life, she is going through a lot. I don't know what else to do. I am really worried about her."

"Well, if that's what you think she needs, fine. But Charles will need to be told." And that was all he was going to say on the subject.

Sharon said, while she was lifting her cup of coffee to take a sip, "I'll tell Charles, I just don't know how."

Bill, a very well-respected child psychiatrist and very good friend of the family, arrived about 2:00 that afternoon. From what he was told by Sharon, he too was concerned about Sharise. When he arrived, Sharise was playing with her building blocks in the front yard. She stopped and ran into the house. "Gramma! There's a strange man here."

Sharon looked up from her knitting and said, "Oh, that's a friend of gramma's. He's actually here to help you."

"O.k. gramma, but he doesn't look like he can build a castle any better than you can."

Sharon chuckled, "He's not here to help you with your castle. He's here to talk to you about your mommy and daddy."

"Oh." Sharise said very disappointed. She would much rather have someone that can build a castle. It seems like everyone wanted to talk to her about her mommy and daddy, but no one can build a descent castle.

Bill walked up to Sharise. "You must be Sharise."

"Yes. My gramma said you want to help me. She also said you can't make a good castle either."

He laughed. "She's right. I am here to help you, and I don't do well with castles. I do need to talk to your gramma and grampa first. I will come and get you when it's your turn."

"Gramma, can I watch a movie while you talk?"

"Ok, but keep it down and remember, you may not get through it all before Bill is ready to talk to you so don't get upset if you have to stop in the middle of it."

"O.K."

Sharise went into the house to watch a movie and Bill sat down with Sharon and Jack.

"Sharon, you said Sharise lost her mother a few months ago and her father just married someone that she hates, is that about right?"

"That's about right. I don't care for her either. No one is as sweet as she pretends to be. She pushed herself into Sharise's life and is just making it miserable for this little girl. I can't stand by and do nothing. I hope you can help her."

"I will do my best. She is also having nightmares, right?"

"Yes, she had one last night. I'm really worried."

"Do you know what they are about?"

"Her mother. She always wakes up screaming, 'mommy, I want my mommy.'"

Bill looked up from his note pad, "Don't you think that's understandable. It's only been eight months since her mom died. That's actually quite normal. I will talk to her and see if I can help her get over the nightmares at least."

Sharon called Sharise and "Sharise, Bill is ready to talk to you."

Sharise came in a little upset, she was a little upset since she didn't get to finish her movie. "Already, gramma? I haven't hardly even started my movie yet."

"Sharise...I told you Bill was here to help you. You can finish your movie later. Just tell him how you feel. *Exactly* how you feel. No matter what it is you want to say, you can trust him."

"ok, gramma. But I don't think he will like what I have to say." She said with her head hung down. She followed Bill into the house so they could have some privacy. Sharon and Jack stayed out on the porch. Bill and Sharise hit it off right away. They talked for a couple of hours. They talked about everything from building castles to Sharise's feelings about her mom's death and her dad's marriage to Monica. After they were done, Bill told Sharise that he needed to talk to her grandparents again. She said, "Ok." And went to get them. When Sharon and Jack came in, they sat down and Sharon started the conversation. "Well, do you think you can help her, is she ok? What's wrong with her? What has that woman done to her?"

"Sharon," Bill said, "I don't think that Monica has done anything to her. Although she is likely not her best friend. You have a beautiful granddaughter and she is very sensitive. Her feelings for her father are very strong... this is why she has a problem with Monica. She's jealous. For three months she had only you two and her father, then all of a sudden, he brings someone else into the home and she is feeling threatened. She is worried about losing her father to her. She is scared and doesn't know how to deal with her emotions. The only feelings she really understands are love, and hate. Since she doesn't love her, she thinks she must hate her. She doesn't understand anything in between. The two emotions are so closely related, that if she is not careful, she will wind up hating her father. The main reason she lashes out at Monica is she doesn't know what else to do. She's already lost her mother and doesn't want to lose her father too. she will likely outgrow this stage. However, as I explained to her, I think she needs to begin regular visits with me. I think that if she has an outlet, some place to release her anger, you know, someone without an emotional connection, maybe she won't hate Monica so much. It's going to be a rocky ride, but if she responds, it will be well worth it."

Sharon didn't like that last statement. "What do you mean if?"

Bill explained, "Although it's very uncommon for children not to respond, there is a possibility that she will never get over this. She may continue with the jealousy and hatred into her adulthood. I don't see that happening, but you need to be prepared for it."

Sharon stood there with a look of disbelief. "*What if this doesn't work?*" she thought, "*it could ruin her life. I really hate this woman.*" She looked over at Bill and said, "I don't know if *I* will ever outgrow *my* feelings about Monica, but I don't have to live with her."

Bill began gathering his papers and note pads. As he was picking up the last of them, he looked over at Sharon and said to her in a very stern voice, "I would also like to talk to you about that. For Sharise's sake you need to try your best to be nice to Monica. I know you don't like her either, and we will be discussing that the next time I am here, but you must do your very best to avoid speaking ill of her. Especially in front of Sharise. You must promise me, Sharon."

Sharon did not respond to him immediately. "Sharon….?'"

She finally dropped her head and said, "Ok, Bill. I will do my best…. but only around Sharise. Her well-being is more important to me than anything else. I won't promise not to speak my mind when Sharise is not here."

"I guess I can't ask for more than that. I'll see you in a couple of weeks. I will call you later this week to set up the next session. Make sure you let her dad know." Bill said as he started for the door.

"Of course, and thank you." Sharon said as she walked him to the door. After Bill left, she looked over at Jack, who hadn't so much as coughed throughout the entire conversation and, shaking her head, said, "See, Jack, I told you she was ok. I don't know why you insisted I call Bill. Let's all go out to dinner tonight."

Jack just shook his head, "Yes, dear." That was his most frequent response to his wife. He figured that it kept him out of trouble. He was probably right.

The next few days went very well. Sharise didn't have any nightmares, and Monica's name seldom came up in conversation. When she did, Sharon was as positive about her as she could. She did not want to be the cause of Sharise getting worse. She didn't like the woman any more than before, but she also didn't want the nightmares to come back.

When Charles and Monica returned, Sharon was very nice to her. Sharise had decided to try to get along with her and even gave Monica a weak hug. She didn't run up to her dad the way she had before, but she was glad to see him. She had so much to tell him. "Daddy, can we go home now?"

Charles and Monica were both a bit surprised about the turn around Sharise had made.

"Is this my little angel back? I am really glad to see you acting like such a big girl. We'll go home in the morning ok? It is late and we are very tired."

"Ok daddy, I'm a little tired too. Can I sleep with you tonight?" Sharise said with a yawn.

"I don't think so, Honey. That bed is not quite big enough for the three of us." Charles said as he gave his little girl a big hug. Sharise was very disappointed. She hadn't seen her father for several days and really missed him.

"But daddy, I just want to spend some time with you on your first night back. I missed you." She said softly.

Charles was about to repeat his earlier refusal when Monica interrupted, "Charles, it's only for one night. I don't mind if you don't. I can sleep in her bed for one night."

Charles looked down at little Sharise, she had turned on the charm. She was staring up at him with a look that he just couldn't resist. He looked at her with loving eyes and said, "Ok, but just one night. I mean it little lady, just for tonight. This isn't going to be a regular thing."

Sharise smiled the biggest smile Charles had seen in a long time. With her eyes lit up she said, "Thank you, daddy. I love you so much. I gotta get the puppy you got me out of my room…" she paused for a moment and dropped her head as she said, "unless Monica wants to sleep with him." She looked at Monica hoping she would say no. Sharise was not really ready to share her dog with a woman she still didn't like, but she also wanted to make her daddy happy.

Monica was a bit surprised. She really didn't expect Sharise to even consider sharing the dog that her father had given her. She thought about it for a moment and decided to test Sharise to find out if she is sincere or just trying to make her father happy. She was sure that Sharise still hated her, and she wanted to show Charles the truth about his daughter. "I would love it if you would be willing to share your dog with me. That way, I won't be so lonesome. I really appreciate your generosity." She looked at Sharise with a little evil look making sure that Charles didn't see it.

Sharise definitely saw it. She knew that Monica was only doing this to be mean, and it really hurt her. But, she thought as she fought back the tears, she was going to be sleeping with her dad and as long as Monica didn't hurt the stuffed dog, then she would be ok. If she did do something to hurt him, then her daddy would take care of it. Either way, she would be ok. "Ok, but he likes to sleep on the side nearest the window. And don't squeeze him too hard, cause he is very sentative." She said regretfully. Then she looked up at her daddy, hoping for a nod of approval. He gave her the nod and a smile.

The next morning Sharise slept in a little. Sharon decided she needed to let Charles know about Bill, but wasn't quite sure how. So, as they sat at the kitchen table, she started getting a little fidgety. She got up, walked over to the refrigerator to get cream, then got up and got sugar, then got up and just walked over to the refrigerator, open the door, look around for a while and then closed the door. Then she walked back over to the table, sat down, then got up again, walked over to the counter, looked around, and then came back to the table and sat down. She was just about to tell him when Monica walked in.

"I hope you slept well Charles. That bed that Sharise sleeps in is the most uncomfortable thing I have ever slept in." she said as she rubbed the back of her neck. "I will be glad to get home and sleep in a good bed." She sat at the table and looked at Sharon as if to say 'where's breakfast?' Sharon saw the look and sweetly said, "Sorry you missed breakfast, but that's what happens when you sleep too long." She then walked out of the kitchen.

Monica looked at Charles and said, "now that was uncalled for. I didn't say anything about breakfast. Although it would have been a nice gesture." She then got up and got a cup of coffee and went out on the front porch by herself.

Shortly after that, Sharise got up, got herself some cereal and sat next to her daddy. "Where's Gramma?" she asked with a mouth full of cereal.

Charles looked down at her and said, "I am not sure, she is here somewhere and don't talk with your mouth full, young lady."

"Sorry Daddy." She finished the rest of her breakfast quietly, set her bowl in the sink and sat on Charles' lap. Charles looked down at her with loving eyes and told her to go upstairs and get dressed and ready to go. She hopped down and did as her daddy said.

On the way home, Sharise decided she should tell her daddy about Bill. "Daddy?"

"Yes."

"Gramma had a man come over to talk to me. She said he was a psychotic and could help me."

Charles and Monica looked at each other with confusion. Then Charles realized what she meant. "I think you mean a 'psychiatrist'" They both started laughing. Sharise did not think it was funny at all. She thought they were making fun of her. Charles glanced in the rear-view mirror and saw the little girl he loved so much almost in tears. "I'm sorry honey. We weren't laughing at you. We were laughing because it was so cute. It's good to try new words even if you don't get them right the first time. Now tell me about this psychiatrist, did he help you?"

"I think so. He said…." she paused unsure if she should go on.

Charles was a little concerned now. "What did he tell you Sharise? Was it bad?"

"No. It was about Monica."

"Charles," Monica broke in, "I think she's afraid that I'll get angry. Maybe you should talk about this another time, when the two of you are alone."

"No," Charles said, "Sharise, Monica is part of our family now, there are to be no secrets. What did he say?"

Sharise looked over at Monica, she wasn't afraid of hurting her feelings, she was only worried about upsetting her father. Slowly she began, "He told me that I don't like Monica because she's trying to take you away from me. He called it 'jelsy' or somthin like that. He said she wasn't trying to do that, but in the back of my brain that's what I'm scared of. We talked about you and mommy and gramma and grampa and even the puppy I always wanted. He said I was o.k. and the stuff I'm feeling is espected. He said that I had to try really hard to like Monica because she is going to be around for a long time and it would make it lots easier if I do. He also said he wants to see me again to make sure I am doing the stuff he told me to."

"Well, it sounds like he helped you understand *why* you hate me," Monica said, "But do you think he helped you get *over* your hatred towards me?"

Sharise thought for a few moments. "He said I don't I hate you. I just don't know you. I'm gonna try real hard to like you."

"Well, I am proud of you honey. I know Monica will be there for you anytime you need her. I'm glad you two worked things out." Charles said as he smiled at Sharise through the rear-view mirror.

Not much was said the rest of the way home. Sharise still didn't like Monica and Monica knew it, but she did tell her daddy that she would try. The next few hours were a little tense – no one would break the silence until they arrived home.

Charles looked back at Sharise, "Honey, we're home. Stay in the car for just a minute, we have a surprise for you. I want to make sure it's ready," He and Monica got out of the car and went inside. Tony, Charles best friend, was waiting for them. "It's all set up in the back yard, Chucky Boy. You guys are later than I thought."

"I know; we were delayed at lunch. Sharise kinda took her time. If she knew what was waiting for her, she wouldn't have wanted to even stop. You two go back there, I'll get Sharise." He had a hard time keeping in his excitement as he walked to the car to get his little girl. "Come on, Honey, let's go see your surprise."

Sharise was also excited. She couldn't imagine what it could be. Her birthday wasn't for a week. "What is it Daddy? Will I like it? Tell me Daddy, tell me."

"I'll do better than tell you, I'll show you. But you have to close your eyes. And keep them closed, ok?"

"O.K. Daddy." He held onto her hand and led her into the house and to the back door. As he slid open the glass door, Sharise was having a hard time keeping her eyes closed. She had to hold her hand over her eyes. Charles sat his little angel down on the wrought iron bench in the garden. "Keep your eyes closed." Charles reminded her. Then he motioned to Tony. Suddenly she felt a cold nose and warm tongue on her cheek. She opened her eyes and squealed with delight. There, staring her in the face, was the most beautiful cocker spaniel puppy she'd ever seen. "Daddy! A puppy! It's just what I always wanted. Thank you Daddy!" Sharise gave her father a big hug and kiss.

"Sharise, honey, it was Monica's idea. She didn't want to wait for your birthday. She felt you were kind of feeling left out after the wedding, so she thought now would be the perfect time."

Sharise slowly walked over to Monica and gave her a reluctant hug. "Thank you, Monica."

"You're welcome, Sharise. Why don't you go play with your puppy?"

Tony was holding the puppy's leash. "I think your puppy needs a name little lady." Tony always called her that. Sometimes she wondered if he knew her real name.

"Is it a girl dog or a boy dog?" Tony looked at the puppy.

"It's a girl."

"Then her name will be Princess."

"That's perfect." Sharise and Tony played with Princess for several hours. Monica and Charles watched, very pleased with the decision to get the puppy.

"It's time to go in Sharise. It's getting late."

"Can Princess come in Daddy? Please?"

"Ok, but you have to keep an eye on her. If she potties in the house, you have to clean it up. Understand?"

"Yes, Daddy. I know. I have to clean up the poopy."

Sharise and Princess were inseparable until school started again. As soon as Sharise got home from school, they were together again. Princess even "helped" Sharise with her homework. The following few weeks were somewhat uneventful. Sharise did everything she could to get along with Monica. Charles did most of his work at home. With the exception of the rare court appearance that no one else from his office could handle. Everything seemed to be going along just fine until the report card arrived. Sharise was very proud of herself. She only got one "B". Her father was equally proud, but Monica did not approve. "How can you think she is doing her best when she received a "B"? You know she is capable of straight "A"s. I'm not real pleased with her achievement, or should I say, lack thereof." Sharise was very confused. She thought she did really well. Who does this woman think she is, butting in like that? she thought. Oh well, Daddy is proud of me anyway. That's what counts.

"Maybe you're right Monica. Sharise? Honey, why are you getting a "B" in math? Are you sure you're trying your very best?"

Sharise couldn't believe it. Her father was taking Monica's side. What was so bad about a "B"? She'd done worse than that before and he never got mad. Last year she hadn't received a single "A". She got all "B"s and "C"s. She thought she had done really well, and so did her dad until *she* stepped in and opened her mouth. Monica had succeeded in turning her daddy against her, at least this time. Sharise ran off to her room crying hysterically. She couldn't believe that her daddy was acting this way. Apparently, the only friend she had in this house was Princess. She stayed in her room all night. She didn't even come out for dinner. From that point on, she decided not to try so hard to like 'Demonica'. After all, her daddy was proud of her until she 'put a spell on him'.

Charles had to go to court a few days later and would be gone all evening. Sharise did not want to be alone with 'Demonica'. "Daddy, can I go to Tony's house after school today? Jessie and I could play together. She hasn't even seen Princess yet. Maybe I could bring her with me."

"No, Sharise. You need to stay here after school. You'll have homework and you can't take Princess to school with you. I'm sorry, but the answer has to be no."

"But, Daddy, it's Friday and I never have homework on Friday. Maybe Tony could pick us up. Then I wouldn't have to leave her here all by herself."

"She won't be by herself because you will be here with her."

"Please, Daddy, please? I love you bunches."

Charles looked into her pleading eyes. "I'll tell you what, if Monica will take you, you can go. But *you* have to ask her. I have to go to work now," he said as he kissed her forehead. "Good-bye my little angel."

"Good-bye, Daddy." Sharise really didn't want to ask Monica for anything, but she also didn't want to spend the entire evening alone with her.

"Monica, would you take me and Princess to Tony's house after school today? Daddy said I could go if you took me. Please?"

Monica glared hatefully at this tiny child, "What do you think I am, your personal taxi service? If you want to go, you'll have to find your own way there."

Sharise looked very disappointed. "But, Daddy said I could only go if you took me. Jessie hasn't seen princess yet, and I thought maybe you'd take us over there."

"Well, you thought wrong!! I don't even like that dog. You think I'm going to let her into my car? Forget it!! Call Tony. If he will come and get you, then you can go. I don't want you *or* that dog around tonight, but if he won't pick you up, I'm sure not taking you."

"But my daddy said…"

"Well…your daddy's not here, is he? That means I'm the boss. If you want to go, you'll call Tony."

"Ok, but if my daddy gets mad it's not my fault."

Monica glared at her, "I'll take care of your daddy."

Tony agreed to picked them up after school. They were having so much fun, they lost track of time. At about 10:00 Charles called. "Tony, is my daughter there?"

"Sure. Sharise, it's your dad."

Sharise looked at the clock. "Oh no! I was supposed to be home at 8:00!" She ran to pick up the phone. "Hi, Daddy. I'm sorry. We were having so much fun…"

"You are in deep trouble young lady!! I told you you couldn't go unless Monica took you. She's been very worried about you. I'm on my way to pick you up. You'd better be ready." He hung up the phone before Sharise even had a chance to defend herself. She slowly hung up the phone and began to cry. Demonica had won again.

When Charles arrived, Sharise and Tony both tried to explain what happened, but he was so angry, he wouldn't listen to either one of them. Now Sharise was very angry, not only at Monica, but at her father as well. He didn't believe a word she said. He called her a liar. She began to cry again on the way home. "Please, Daddy, please believe me. I told her you said I couldn't go unless she took me, but she said she was the boss and she'd take care of things with you. She said she didn't want me or Princess around tonight. I'm sorry Daddy, I'm sorry."

"You're going to be very sorry young lady! You will remain in your room for the rest of the weekend. That means no going shopping with Monica, no friends over, no video games, and no playing with Princess. You'll clean your room and only come out to use the bathroom and eat dinner. Is that understood?"

"Yes, Daddy." She understood alright. Monica was taking over and really messing things up. Worst of all, there was nothing she could do about it. She wasn't real upset about not going shopping with Monica, but no Princess? That was the worst. How could her daddy believe that *woman* over his own daughter? She hated her before, but now she really despised her. She's not even sure if she likes her father anymore. After all, he only listens to *Monica*. They used to be very close, but now she didn't even know him. When they pulled into the garage, Sharise went straight to her room. She decided it was time to call Gramma Sharon. She'd believe her. She knew she could always count on Gramma. The only problem was; she couldn't leave her room. Or could she? They have to sleep sometime. She decided that after they went to sleep, she'd sneak out of her room and make the call.

It was about midnight and they were still up. Sharise was having a difficult time staying awake. Finally, at about 1:30, they went to sleep. "Gramma will be asleep." She thought. "This is important, she'll understand." She tip-toed out of her room. She knew if she got caught, she'd be in even more trouble. She didn't care. Somebody has to believe her. Gramma was her only hope. Just as she reached for the phone, her father came in the room. "Sharise? What are you doing out of your room?"

Sharise thought for a moment. "I was... thirsty. I need a drink of water. I thought you were asleep. I didn't want to wake you. I'm sorry. I'll go back to my room." She turned to leave the kitchen when her father stopped her.

"Did you get your drink?"

"No."

"Here, let me get it for you." Sharise thought she was in more trouble, but her dad just got her water and sent her back to bed. Now she'd have to wait until tomorrow. Oh well, she was tired anyway. Maybe when Monica went shopping, she could make her call.

She slept in the following morning. By the time she got up, Monica had already left, and her father was working in his office in the back part of the house. This was her opportunity. She went into the kitchen and called her grandma. She told her the whole story. "I'll be there in a few hours to talk to your father. This is ridiculous. Go on back to your room so you don't get into any more trouble. Grandma will take care of everything."

Sharise hung up the phone just as her father was entering the kitchen. "You're up. Good. How about some breakfast."

Sharise was still a little frightened. She thought he heard her talking to her grandmother. She hoped if she acted like nothing happened, maybe he wouldn't know. "Bacon, eggs and pancakes?"

"Sorry, I don't think I have time for all that. How about bacon, eggs, and toast?"

"Ok, then can I come out of my room? I'll be good. I promise."

Charles looked at her with sincere affection, "No. you really had us worried last night. No one knew where you were. You can't do that. Did you know that Monica was just about to call the police? She thought you had been kidnapped. She was really concerned. Why did you do that? That's not like you. What's wrong with you?"

Sharise knew that he wouldn't believe the truth. She tried to tell him last night. He wouldn't listen then, why should he listen to her now. She decided on the best answer she could think of, "I don't know, Daddy. I shouldn't have gone. I'm sorry. I thought Monica knew where I was. I'll never do that again. I promise." She almost started to cry again.

"Well, I think you need to spend a little more time in your room. You have to be punished. You know that, don't you?"

"I guess so. Can I wait until after breakfast?" she asked as she gave him a look that she knew her Daddy could not refuse.

Charles smiled, he knew that he was being played, "I suppose so." He made her breakfast and told her not to take too much time eating. He went back into his office. Sharise finished her breakfast and returned to her room. She felt a little bit better knowing at least her grandma believed her. All she had to do is wait for Gramma to show up and she would convince her dad.

A few hours later, just as she promised, Sharon showed up. "Charles!? I understand you have that little angel of yours locked up in her room because of something *that* woman said! How dare you!? How dare you take the word of a woman you have only known a short time over that of your own flesh and blood? How dare you Charles Jackson Sloan!? How dare you! You took the word of a virtual stranger over hers??? What's wrong with your head? Maybe I should have had Bill talk to you instead of Sharise. Did you even talk to Tony? NO!! you just sent her to her room without even hearing her side of the story! Did you even think about her feelings? I seriously doubt it! How could you? I know I taught you better than that. What's wrong with you? I am taking her home with me! Pack her things and have her ready within the hour!"

Charles was astonished. "Mom? How did you know?"

"I'm the gramma, I know everything that goes on here. Now pack her things. Or do I need to do it myself?

"Wait just a minute, Mom. Sharise called you, didn't she? She's in real trouble now!"

"Charles, she had every right to call me. It seems as I'm the only one that believes her. She is not to be punished for trying to get her side of the story told."

"Mom, you better listen to me for a change. She's my daughter and I will deal with this *my* way! You weren't here last night when Monica was crying because she didn't know where Sharise was. She thought she had been kidnapped or something worse. You didn't see the relieved look on her face when I found her at Tony's. you have no right to come in here and take my daughter from me. No right at all!!! How dare you even think about it?!"

"Charles, all I am asking you to do to stop me from taking her away is to find out the truth. For example, why did Monica wait until after 10:00 at night to start worrying? Why didn't *she* call Tony? That would be the rational thing to have done, right? Why wait until you got home to turn on the tears and concern? Why don't you call Tony and find out exactly what went on? Charles, the truth is you weren't here either. You know less about what happened than I do. I listened to Sharise. You should too."

Charles was angry, but decided to appease his mother. "O.k., fine. I will call Tony right now." He went to the phone and dialed the number.

Tony's wife Becky answered. "Hello?"

"Hey Becky. Is Tony there?"

"Charles? He's supposed to be with you. He left here about two hours ago. He said he had something to straighten out. Charles, I'm worried. He should have been there by now, something must have happened. Would you go see if you can find him? I will call the office and see if he stopped by there and got delayed."

"Absolutely I'll go. I'm sure he's alright. I'll call you when I find him. My mom will be here, if you hear from him and can't reach me on my cell, call her at the house, OK?"

"Ok. Please, Charles, you have to find him. It's not like him to change his plans without checking in."

"I'll find him, Becky. I promise." Charles hung up the phone. "Mom, I have to go. Tony's supposed to be here. Becky is worried. He left two hours ago, it's only twenty minutes from his house here. I'm going to look for him. Please stay here and keep an eye on Sharise. And please don't go anywhere until I get back. Promise me?"

"I promise. I won't go anywhere until you get back… go find Tony."

Charles ran out of the house in a panic. He was not at all sure that Tony was ok. He raced down the road. About 5 miles away he saw Tony's car. It was upside down in a ditch. He called 911, then went down to see if he could help his best friend. Tony's arm was hanging out the driver's side window, he was unconscious, Charles wasn't even sure if he was alive. He grabbed his bloody arm and checked for a pulse. He found it! Strong and steady. It seemed like forever before the emergency crews arrived. They removed him from the mangled car, he was still unconscious, but alive. They took him by helicopter to the hospital. Charles followed behind the returning ambulance. Once he arrived at the hospital, he called Becky and told her what happened.

"Call my mom and have her bring you and Sharise to the hospital. You are in no condition to drive." He told her.

Becky did as he asked. Soon, she, Sharon, and Sharise were by Charles' side. "Charles, do they know what happened yet? Is he alright? What's going on? Where is he?" Becky was hysterical and began sobbing. Charles grabbed her and Sharise and held them close.

"He's still in surgery. They're not sure how it happened yet. Lloyd is at the scene now. They don't know how bad Tony's injuries are yet. He did receive head and neck injuries, but his vitals were still very strong when they took him into surgery. The doctors are optimistic that he will be ok."

Sharise looked up at her father with tears in her eyes, "Daddy, is uncle Tony going to sleep like Mommy did?"

Charles reached down and picked up his little angel, "no Honey, not like mommy."

Sharise started crying so hard her whole body shook. "It's all my fault!!! If I hadn't went to his house last night, this wouldn't have happened."

Becky reached over and placed her hand on Sharise's back rubbing lightly. "Look, Little Lady, uncle Tony would not like to hear you talking like that. He loves you very much and would be very upset if he heard you say that. It's not your fault. It was an accident. That's all."

Tony was in surgery for several hours. Charles called Monica to tell her what happened. She wasn't at home, so he left her a message. She arrived just as Tony was getting out of surgery. The doctor came in and asked to speak with Becky alone. "Your husband has been through a lot he has several broken ribs and his back is broken. We've done all we can. It's up to him now. He is stable and in recovery…there is one other thing, he will probably never walk again." Becky started sobbing uncontrollably. Some tears of joy and relief that he is going to be ok, some were tears of fear and anger that he would be paralyzed. Once she calmed down a little, she came out of the room, walked straight to Charles and started crying again. Charles held her and just let her cry. Monica had an angry look on her face, Sharise saw the look, but didn't say anything. She didn't want to upset Becky.

Monica regained her composure and was able to manage a look of compassion. "I'm sorry, Becky. I didn't know Tony very well. Charles said he was a good man."

Becky lifted her head from Charles' shoulder and looked at Monica with anger, tears still streaming down her face, "Monica, he's not dead! The doctor said he would probably be fine, except…." she dropped her head for a moment. Charles reached down and gently grabbed her chin lifting her head up. "Except what?" he asked as he looked into her eyes, red as beets from the tears. "…except that he will probably never walk again." She began sobbing again. Charles pulled her close to him and held her again. She grabbed him as if she would never let him go. Monica watched, her jealousy building.

"What about Jessie, Daddy? Where's Jessie?" Sharise asked. Becky had totally forgotten about her. She couldn't remember where Tony was taking her. Jessie was Tony's daughter from a previous marriage. Was she at her mother's house or her grandmothers? Maybe neither. She couldn't remember. She called Jessie's mother first. Sure enough, she was there. Becky explained everything that happened and asked her to bring Jessie to the hospital. By the time she got there, Tony was awake and the doctors said that Becky could see him. He was awake, although still a little groggy. Sharon hadn't wanted to say anything in front of Becky after all she had just been through, but now was the perfect time to ask a question that had been eating at her. "Monica, what made you think that Tony was dead?" Sharon still did not trust her son's wife, she was absolutely convinced that Monica had something to do with the accident. After all, Tony was Charles' best friend, and anything that took Charles away from Monica, even for a short time, seemed to be a threat.

"Well, it was a terrible accident. His car was upside down in a ditch, totally destroyed. One would only expect the worst. When I saw Becky's reaction after talking to the doctor, I thought that confirmed it. I am so glad that I was wrong. I would hate for anything bad to happen to anyone, but especially someone so close to our family." Monica answered.

Sharon didn't believe it. "Better luck next time." She said under her breath. Sharise heard it, but she was the only one. She wasn't sure what Gramma meant, but she knew she didn't want anyone else to hear it, so now was not a good time to ask. No one had noticed that Becky had come out of Tony's room, just in time to hear Monica's answer to Sharon's question, however since she didn't hear the question, she was kind of confused about what Monica was saying. Charles was also a bit confused, he didn't give Monica any details, just that Tony was in the hospital. He never even mentioned an accident. She wouldn't even have driven by the accident scene. So, how did she know? Becky looked at Monica for just a moment, with a look of anger, she didn't like Monica either. She knew what happened and why Sharise got in trouble for coming to their house. She knew that Monica was aware of where Sharise was and was just trying to cause problems. What she didn't know is why? She looked back at Charles, "Tony is awake and wants to see everyone, but the doctor said he's not quite strong enough. He said that Tony's condition needs to stabilize a bit more before he is allowed visitors outside the family. He didn't say much to me; he doesn't remember the accident. I hope Lloyd found something. Whoever caused this should pay." Becky started to cry again. Charles put his arms around her and Jessie. "I promise that whoever caused this, will pay."

Monica shook her head. "Charles, did the thought ever occur to you that this may have just been a one car accident? Maybe there is no responsible party. Maybe Tony fell asleep or just plain lost control of the car. Maybe it was mechanical failure. You won't know anything until the police report is completed. Just because your wife died at the hands of a drunk driver, doesn't mean that this is the same thing."

Charles looked at her with disbelief. "How do you know Jamie was killed by a drunk driver. The police never found any evidence to support that. Just that it was a possible hit and run. I suspected that it was a drunk driver, but I never said anything to you about it."

Becky chimed in, "Yeah, and how did you know so much about my husband's accident? I was there when Charles called you. He never mentioned any details about the accident, just that Tony was in the hospital. How did you know so much about it?"

Monica became very defensive. "Well, I read about Jamie's accident in the paper. When something like that happens, it makes the news. They suggested the possibility of a drunk driver. I didn't know until later that it was Charles' wife. As for Tony's accident, I talked to the nurse's station. It's not difficult to find information if you know who to ask and how to ask them."

Charles felt a little foolish. He'd practically accused the woman he loved of murder, conspiracy to commit murder and attempted murder based solely on circumstantial evidence. He knew better. "I'm sorry. With everything that has happened in the past twenty-four hours, I guess I am a little touchy. Becky, I think we all should go on home. There is nothing more we can do here. I'll get with Lloyd tomorrow and see what I can find out."

"You go on ahead, Charles. Thank you, but I think I'll stay with Tony tonight in case he wakes up again. The nurse said she would make up a bed in his room for me tonight. Do me a favor and take Jessie with you. She needs to be with friends right now. Charles gave her a hug and said, "no problem. Come on guys, let's go home. I'm sure if there are any changes, they'll call. Becky, call me when you're ready to come home. One of us will pick you up."

Becky had only been awake a few minutes when the police arrived the next morning. "Mrs. Webster." The officer said as he stepped into Tony's room.

"Yes?"

"We're here to ask you a few questions about your husband's accident. Do you have any idea how it might have happened?"

"No, I was at home at the time."

"Tony was alone in the car?"

"Yes. As far as I know."

"Are you sure?"

"Well, he had Jessie in the car with him earlier, but he dropped her off at her mother's house before the accident. Why?"

The officer hesitated. "What color is your daughter's hair?"

"Red. Why? What's going on? Why are you asking me all these questions?"

"We found evidence that there was someone else in the car with him. There were long blonde hairs stuck in one of the screws of the headrest on the passenger side of the car. We've sent them to the lab for analysis. Is there anyone else you can think of that might have been in the car with him?"

Becky thought for a moment, "No. No one that I can think of. What does this mean?"

"We don't know anything for sure. We have to investigate all possibilities. Was there anything wrong with the vehicle that you are aware of? Maybe the brakes, steering, that sort of thing?"

"No. Not that I am aware of. Tony keeps it in pretty good condition. He had the oil changed frequently and the tires checked regularly. The only thing I am aware of is a small dent in the rear of the front bumper where it was hit in a parking lot. Tony almost had a fit over that."

"Ok, what about enemies? Does Tony have any enemies that might want to see him hurt or worse?"

Becky looked at him like he was crazy. "Look, officer, he is a prosecuting attorney. I am sure that there is more than one sick degenerate that is angry enough to want him dead, but most of them are still in prison. As far as a list of names, I'm afraid I can't help you. I don't have any personal knowledge of anyone in particular that would want him dead. Tony is a very kind, loving man that would give you the shirt off his back in the dead of winter if you needed it. He's a wonderful husband and a loving father. I only know a few of his friends and they are all attorney's or law enforcement. Now, if you don't mind, I would like to take a shower, brush my teeth and get dressed. Why don't you go find whoever is responsible for this and leave me alone?" With that she turned and headed to the sink to get her toothbrush and get cleaned up.

The officer grabbed her shoulder, gently, "I am sorry, Mrs. Webster, but we do have a few more questions for you."

Becky swung around she was now very angry. "Look, you guys give me one hour to get cleaned up and I will gladly answer all your questions. Right now, I need a shower and a very strong cup of coffee. It has been a very long night."

The officer removed his hand, "Of course, Mrs. Webster. We'll see you in an hour."

"Fine. Thank you."

Charles arrived just as Becky was finishing getting dressed. "Charles, I'm so glad you're here. The police were here earlier asking a bunch of questions about some blonde that they think was in the car with Tony. They said they found hairs in the screws of the passenger side headrest. Who would have been in the car with him? He dropped off Jessie at her mother's house, then headed to your house. He never goes in to Elsie's house. He refuses to pick up strangers, so it had to be someone he knows. Charles, I am really scared. Who would want to see Tony dead?'

Charles put his arms around her. She buried her head in his chest and began sobbing. "Calm down. It'll be alright." He pulled her away from him and looked her in the eyes, "I promise. Now, did they send the hairs to the lab?"

"Yes." She answered between sobs.

"Good. What else did they say?" He asked as he gently guided her to the chair by Tony's bed.

"Well," she paused, "they asked about the mechanical condition of the car, and if I knew anyone that would want to see him dead. I told them, of course, that as a prosecuting attorney, he likely had many enemies. They also said that they had more questions and would be back in about an hour. That was about forty-five minutes ago. How can they find who was responsible for the accident if they are in here questioning me? I don't know anything."

Charles looked at her with deep compassion, "They're just doing their jobs. Part of the investigation is questioning those closest to the victim. I am a little curious as to why they think that someone is trying to kill him. From what you said they don't have much evidence to support that. Was there anything else they said…." Charles was interrupted by a voice in the doorway.

"Wrong again Mr. Prosecutor." It was Lloyd.

"Lloyd, I've been trying to reach you all morning."

"I know, Charles. I got your messages, all fifteen of them. And all before 9:00 am. I'm impressed." He then turned to Becky. "Mrs. Webster, this is one of the most difficult times to answer questions, I know that. But we need to ask them to be able to understand the whole story. Was Tony taking any drugs that you are aware of?"

Becky looked totally perplexed as she glanced at Charles then back at Lloyd, then back at Charles, "I have a hard time getting him to take an aspirin, Charles you know that." She then looked back to Lloyd, "Why are you asking me this? Tony doesn't do drugs of any kind and I resent the insinuation!!" She said as she stood and faced Lloyd with daggers in her eyes.

"Becky," Charles said in a calming voice, "please, Lloyd is only doing his job. Remember they don't know Tony like we do."

Becky sat back down and placed her head in her hands and began sobbing again. "I'm sorry, I just don't know how to handle all this. One minute everything is going great and the next, my whole life is turned upside down. You never think this kind of thing will happen to you." She said as she lifted her head, "Then it does, and, well, you kinda lose it. Lloyd, Tony would never knowingly take any kind of drugs."

Lloyd looked at Charles with a look of unease. He wasn't sure how to continue without infuriating Becky more. He looked back at Becky and began slowly, "Uh…well… there was a small amount of opium found in his blood work. Not enough to do any real harm, just enough to make him very sleepy. That, along with the brakes failing, makes a potentially deadly combination. Tony's a very lucky man." Lloyd paused for a moment and looked back at Charles, then back at Becky before continuing, "The doctors said that a small dose of opium could have been slipped in his coffee or put in his food. It acts fairly quickly and takes a while to wear off. It could have been given to him as much as two hours before the accident or as soon as fifteen minutes before. They have no way of knowing for sure. He was probably not even aware of it." he stopped. There was only one way to say what he had to say and that was just to come to the point. Lloyd had been in this position before, but, it's more difficult with someone you know. "With the exception of you," he said as he looked at Becky, "and of course Jessie, who I think we can rule out, we can find no evidence or indication that there was anyone else with him during that time frame."

Charles stepped between Lloyd and Becky. "What about the blonde hairs you found in the car? Her hair is red. The DNA should at least give you a starting point, right?"

Lloyd lowered his head and shook it. "The only thing that it tells us is that the other person in the vehicle either grows nylon out of their head, or they were wearing a wig. I think the latter is more likely. Don't you Charles?"

"It certainly makes more sense. But who would go to all the trouble of putting on a wig, getting into a car that they had just 'fixed' the brakes on, and slipping him opium? Just to make sure that he gets into an accident that they can't control or make sure that he doesn't survive? If they wanted to kill him and make it look like an accident, there are much better ways. It seems to me that this person either didn't know what they were doing, or they really didn't care if he lived or died." Charles responded. Becky was very confused. She looked at Lloyd, then back at Charles, "So, Charles, where does that leave us now? Back to square one? How do we find out who is trying to kill Tony if the only evidence they have isn't real?" Lloyd put his hand on Charles shoulder. "Charles," he said, "I hope you know a good defense attorney." Becky was shocked, "Lloyd, Charles would never do anything like this!! They are like brothers, even closer. They...." Lloyd interrupted her, "It's not for him, Mrs. Webster." Becky looked at both of them a bit confused. "I don't understand, why would you tell him that if you are not insinuating that he had something to do with it?" Becky asked.

"Lloyd, you are not saying what I think you are saying, are you?" Charles asked. Lloyd just looked away and then looked over to Becky, "Mrs. Webster, you have the right to remain silent anything you say…" Becky burst into tears. She wasn't able to even respond just cry.

Charles couldn't believe what he was seeing, his best friend's wife was being arrested. "Lloyd, what are the charges and on what grounds?"

Lloyd had one of the other officers that was there put the handcuffs on Becky as he himself was not sure if what he was doing was the right thing or not. All he knew was that it was his duty to uphold the law and bring the suspects in, not to judge guilt or innocence. He grabbed Charles and pulled him aside. He wasn't sure if Tony, in the condition that he was, could hear or understand what was going on around him but, he did not want to take any chances of causing any more pain than necessary. "Charles," he began, "based on an anonymous tip, along with the circumstantial evidence we have, we got a warrant to search the Webster's home this morning. When we searched, we found a blonde wig and a small, partially empty bottle of opium in a box hidden in the back of the closet. Unfortunately, that is enough to hold her for the attempted murder of her husband. I really am sorry, Charles, I am." He walked back to where the officers were standing with Becky, "Let's go." He took Becky with them out of the hospital. She kept looking back at Charles hoping that he would stop them, but he couldn't. There was really nothing he could do at that point but watch with disbelief as they continued down the hallway and out the door. He looked back at the room his best friend was lying in and had to figure out whether he would go back in there and tell him what happened, or to go to the police station to try to help Becky. Just then a nurse came walking up to him. "Are you Charles?" she asked. Charles answered her, "Yes." The nurse grabbed his hand gently, "he is asking for you." Charles followed the nurse into Tony's room. Tony lay there, still groggy, he looked at Charles and asked him, "I thought I heard Becky. Where is she. The nurse said she was here, but she left kind of in a hurry. Why did she leave, is she ok?"

Charles wasn't quite sure how to answer him. He really didn't want to tell him that his wife was arrested, he also knew that there was no way around it. He walked up to the bed reached down and put his hand on Tony's shoulder. "She's fine, Tony. Only..." Tony could tell Charles was having difficulty. "Only what, Charles? What's wrong?" Tony begged him with his eyes to tell him. Charles knew he had to let him know. "Tony, she was arrested. They think she had something to do with your accident. They found some evidence in the house that they are saying ties her in with the accident. Is there anything you can remember about the accident? Anything at all?"

Tony couldn't believe what he was hearing. "I can't remember anything about what happened. The last thing I remember was dropping Jessie off at her mother's house. Next thing I know I'm here in the hospital. Charles, what did they find? What could possibly make Lloyd think that Becky would have any reason to hurt me? Has he lost his mind? She would never hurt me." Charles looked him directly in the eyes and said, "Hey buddy, I will take care of Becky, you need to concentrate on remembering what happened. Do you remember picking up Sharise at my house?" Tony shook his head no. He was still sedated a bit and was having some difficulty staying awake. Charles understood that it would take some time for Tony to get his memory back, if at all. He grabbed Tony's hand. "Get some rest. We'll talk more later." He turned to walk out of the room. "Charles?" Tony said. "call John. He's the best defense attorney I know. Tell him…." Tony dozed off. Charles said softly, "I'll tell him, Tony, I'll tell him." He left the hospital and headed home.

Later that morning, Charles called John Stone, an attorney that he and Tony met several years before and were very close friends with. While Tony and Charles became prosecutors, John went to the other side of the bench to become a defense attorney. They each had their motivations, but John seemed to be more passionate about defense, and with good reason. Several years ago, when John was just a boy, his brother, Tom, was arrested for assault. Supposedly, there was a fight and Tom nearly killed a guy. The man that was assaulted was caught with another man's wife, and both families being "prominent" men in the community, they did not want a scandal. They charged Tom with the assault and railroaded him. He wasn't guilty, but by the time the truth came out, Tom had already been arrested, tried, convicted, and sentenced to 10yrs in prison. He was murdered in prison 2 yrs. after he started serving his time. His defense attorney was paid off to withhold evidence that would have cleared him. John was determined not to let anyone else get convicted without proper defense if he could help it. Charles knew he could rely on John to do everything to help Becky with her defense. He also knew that unless Tony remembered at least something about the accident, Becky would be in real trouble. There was no one to corroborate her story. She was alone in the house at the time of the accident. The only thing that she could come close to proving is that she was home after the accident, and Charles wasn't 100% sure about that. He knew how the prosecution thinks and that they will bring up the fact that she could have had the call forwarded to a cell phone. As a prosecuting attorney himself, he knew exactly what they would do and what they would be looking for. John told him that without evidence to the contrary, Becky would have a long hard time explaining where she was and why the items connected to the accident were in her house.

The next several weeks were very difficult for Charles and his family, not to mention Tony and Jessie. Becky was preparing to go through her hearing, which had been postponed a couple of times due to the inability for Tony to remember anything about the incident. He was finally home, but, being confined to a wheelchair didn't help his well-being. He can't remember any more than he could at the hospital, and his wife was in jail for trying to kill him. Jessie was taken to her mother's house so he didn't have to worry about caring for her, and he had a nurse to assist him. Not being able to be with his daughter and read her bedtime stories brought tears to his eyes every night.

John was not able to come up with a suitable defense without Tony's memory. He was almost to the point of believing her guilty…almost. After all, how do you defend a person with no alibi, no witnesses and enough evidence to hang her from the highest tree, circumstantial or not. This was a case that, unless a miracle happened, was virtually impossible to win. John was offered a lesser charge of attempted manslaughter which he was hesitant to discuss, but knew there were not many options left. As he arrived at the jail to meet with her, he hesitated a few moments to try to clear his head a little before he approached her with the offer. He didn't want to even consider it, but he had no other options. As he walked into the room to talk to Becky, he dropped his head a little, he was ashamed to have to have to do what he was about to do. Becky looked at him with a look of confusion and concern. She knew there was something wrong. She stood up, shackles and all, and asked him, "What's wrong John? What's happened?" John finally raised his head and looked her in the eyes, "Becky, I am not sure quite how to say this…." He paused for a few moments. Becky sat down, expecting to hear something horrible had happened to Tony, hoping and praying that the sinking feeling in her stomach was caused by something else. "Becky, the prosecution has offered you a plea bargain. They want you to plead guilty to a charge of attempted manslaughter and assault." He stopped and took a deep breath as Becky just sat there in shock. She couldn't believe that he was even suggesting this. He continued, "I hate to say it, but I think you should take it. I don't know what else to do. Unless your husband can remember something, anything, about the accident, there is nothing to prove your innocence…. I am sorry." Becky just looked at him, she wasn't sure how to respond. Then as she sat there and what he said finally sunk in, she went from shock to anger pretty quickly. "I don't believe what I am hearing. Tony trusts you, he asked you to help me, not hang me. I don't understand why you are even suggesting that I plead guilty to anything. I did not try to kill my husband!! I Love him more than life itself. What ever happened to innocent until *proven* guilty!? You get out of here. And take your 'bargain' with you. I will not say that I am guilty of something I didn't do. I can't believe it. How dare you! How dare you!! Get out!!" she began to cry. John stood up, "Becky, I'm sorry, I don't know what else to do. There are no witnesses to your whereabouts at the time before the accident. The evidence that was found at your house was so incriminating that even Charles has started to doubt your innocence. I'm afraid that unless Tony's memory returns and he can tell us who was in the car with him, we are dead in the water. Don't you get it? You are in deep water and the ship is going down. Your only hope is a plea of guilty. There is no other way out." Becky was infuriated. "No! I will not plead guilty to something I didn't do. Now *you* understand something. I was exactly where I said I was. If you can't help me, then I suggest you find an attorney that can. Now get out before I have the guard take you out." John gathered his things. He did not want to give up on her. She was right, he had to stick to his guns and defend her in the best way he knew how, and not surrender to the opposition, regardless of the odds. He started towards the door, stopped, turned to Becky and said, "Tony asked me to defend you. He had Charles call me because he knows I am the best at what I do. I had to put this option to you to see your reaction. You reacted the way I expected, however, there is little hope of getting you off with the information that I have versus what the prosecution has.

Please understand, that if we continue, we have little hope without Tony's memory." Becky just stood there glaring at him. He then turned and walked away

John went directly to Tony's. As he was arriving, Charles was just leaving. "Charles, how is our boy doing today?" Charles shook his head and dropped his eyes, "I guess he's doing as well as can be expected given the circumstances." He paused a moment, "is there anything you can do for Becky? I mean, without Tony's memory, it doesn't seem to be improving." John shook his head, "It doesn't look good. I was given an offer of a plea bargain…" Charles interrupted, "you didn't take it right? I mean she is not guilty and she will not agree to a plea bargain that even suggests anything else. Tony won't like it either." John just shook his head again. "I presented it to her, but she declined it. I don't know what to do now." Charles just sighed and walked away. Then he stopped. John could see a look of inspiration in his eyes as he turned back. "What about a hypnotist? Maybe that could help? I don't know much about it myself, but I have heard of it helping people recall things that were suppressed." John was not sure about that. "I never put much faith in that stuff, but I will ask him, what can it hurt, right? I have run out of ideas, maybe it will at the very least relax him enough to help him sleep." They both chuckled a little bit. Then Charles walked away and headed home. John continued to the front door there were construction materials in the yard that he had a little difficulty walking over, almost tripping a couple of times. As he walked up to the door, it opened. He heard Tony from inside the home, "Come in, John." John walked through the door with a look of confusion, Tony was nowhere to be seen. "I had the door wired for remote entry and a camera placed so I can see whoever is here and either let them in or…not. I think it is pretty handy. I think I am going to have the whole house wired." He said as he came around the corner into the living room in his wheelchair. "I think I will have it all wired so all I have to do is push a button and the doors open, the toilet flushes and the TV rotates so I can see it. Not all at the same time of course. I could wire the kitchen to make it easier for me to use, but Beck might be a little put out. After all, that is her area of expertise and as soon as she gets home, I won't be in there that much."

John kneeled in front of Tony's chair, not really sure how to tell him his wife may not be home for a very long time. "Tony," he began, "I recommended that she plead guilty to attempted manslaughter." Tony just stared at him, not believing what he was hearing. John wasn't sure what to say next. "Tony? Did you hear what I said? I recommended…" Tony stopped him by grabbing his arm. "I heard what you said John, I just can't believe you said it. Why would you have her take a plea bargain for something you and I both know she didn't do? You can't ask her to do that. She didn't do anything wrong. I don't understand. She didn't agree, did she?" John answered him, "No she didn't agree. I didn't expect her to either. I know in my heart that she had nothing to do with the accident, your being drugged or the brakes being tampered with. But my heart is not going to be on the jury. *I* am not going to be on the jury. Unless you can remember something, *anything* about the accident, she is not in a good position. I don't know what else I can do." John stood up and looked down at Tony. He had his head in his hands, and began to cry. John put his hand on his shoulder

"Ton, I don't know what to say to you, I don't believe she is guilty, you know I don't, I just can't prove it." Tony reached up and gabbed John's hand "I know John, I just wish I could remember." He slammed his fist down on the arm of his chair, "why can't I remember!!" he yelled. John just stood there, helpless. He couldn't even imagine what Tony was going through at this moment. "John, I know there has to be something you can do. She is not guilty. I know she's not. There has to be a witness somewhere. Someone had to have seen something." John stood there for a moment, just looking for something he could say that would help his friend feel at least a little better. He couldn't come up with anything. So, he sat down in a chair across from Tony. They sat there for quite a while. Neither of them really knowing what to say, they just sat and drank coffee. As they sat, John kept trying to come up with a way to present the idea of a hypnotist, but not knowing what to think about it himself, he was having a hard time deciding how to sell the idea to Tony. Tony himself thought as they sat there, he knew his wife was innocent, but couldn't figure out how to prove it. If only there were a way. He looked at his friend sitting there in deep thought. "John?" John looked up from his cup, "Yes, Tony." Tony continued, "John, I have been sitting here thinking. There has to be a way to bring back my memory, a way to help me help my wife. I just can't figure it out. The doctors said my memory may come back, in time." He stopped and stared into his cup for a moment, "She doesn't have that kind of time. I need to remember now. I need to remember…" he started slamming his fist on the arm of the chair again, then he started to hit himself upside the head with both hands on either side. "Why? Why? Why can't I remember?" he started sobbing and continued "Why. Why... why.... why?" John started to talk, then stopped. He wasn't sure if this was the right time or not. He decided not to bring it up. Not yet anyway. So, he just sat there, not saying anything, allowing Tony to let out his anger. After a while, the sobbing came to a slow stop. Tony couldn't cry anymore. He was still angry, but he knew crying wouldn't help...not really. John stood up to leave. Tony stopped him, "John? I don't want Becky to take the offer they made. I know she didn't have anything to do with this accident, but I don't know what to do. If only I could remember what happened that day." John turned back around and looked down at Tony. "There is a possibility, Tony, I don't know if I believe in it, but Charles brought up maybe...." Tony looked at him with begging eyes. "Maybe what?" he said. John shook his head, "Hypnotism. Charles thought that maybe a hypnotist could help you remember. Like I said, I don't know if I believe in it or not, but I don't think it could hurt. What do you think?" Tony didn't know what to think. If he tried it and remembered something that might even slightly be used against his wife, he could never live with himself. On the other hand, he might remember enough to completely exonerate her. "John, if you think it will help, I would do anything to regain my memory. I know she didn't do it, I know it. She was at home. I remember leaving the house with Jessie early in the morning. I think it was about 7:00. She was still in bed. I took jessie to her mother's house and... wait a minute..." Tony had a look on his face as if he was remembering something. Then the look faded. He shook his head. John stooped down to look him in the eyes, "What, Tony, what? Are you remembering something about that day? Keep working on it, keep pushing. You left the house about 7:00, dropped Jessie off at her mom's house…then?" he pushed, trying to get Tony to remember something, anything that might help. "you have to remember. Your wife is counting on it. She needs you now more than ever. Keep trying." Tony looked very confused, he wasn't sure if the memory was even real. "John…" he began, "I don't know…. it's strange, Monica?" John stood back up, "Tony…Tony!" Tony looked up at him, "Huh, what? What was I saying?"

"Tony, you said 'Monica'. What did you mean? What does Monica have to do with it?"

"Monica? I don't know, my mind is like swiss cheese. Or maybe a dream. I remember bits and pieces sometimes, but I don't know if they are even connected. I get so frustrated. I feel like my life is spinning out of control. I don't know what to do."

John shook his head again, "Look, your wife is facing her hearing next week. I have to have something by then or I will have no choice but to go with the plea of guilty, maybe I can get an insanity plea, but probably not. I may be able to push it back a little more, but I don't know how much longer I can do that. We need to have more. The only other choice is up to you." Tony looked at him again confused, "What is the other choice, hypnotism? I don't know about that. I'm not sure if that is something that will work, and even if it does, the court might not accept it. I don't think that is going to be good for Becky. You need to come up with something else. I don't want to put her future in the hands of someone or something that might not help her. There has to be something else. You have got to help her." John said to him, hesitantly, "Becky wants me off the case. She doesn't feel that I am competent enough for her. If you take me off the case, they would have to give her more time for her new defense team to become familiar with her case and do their own analysis of the evidence and put a better defense together for her. I would, of course, turn over everything I have. Unfortunately, there isn't much."

Tony thought about it. He wasn't sure if that would work or not. "If I were to do that, who would you suggest take over? You're the best defense attorney around. You know it and I know it. If you can't prove her innocence, what makes you think someone else…" he paused, "…can?" he finished. He had a strange look on his face. John was not sure what to make of it. Tony looked puzzled, confused and then a blank stare came over him. He shook his head as if he were trying to shake something off of himself. He stopped and stared at nothing again for a moment. Then slowly, he said, "I…I think…I don't know. I keep thinking that Demonica has something to do with this, I can't quite remember…but, she keeps popping into my thoughts, like in a dream…not a good one. I…wish I could pull all my thoughts together. Right now, they are like a damn jigsaw puzzle with pieces missing. Sometimes, you know, I try to remember and get absolutely nothing, other times, just pictures, some people, some places. It's absolutely infuriating." He looked up at his friend and asked, "Would you do something for me?" John was puzzled. "Tony, you know all you have to do is ask. And who is Demonica?"

"Sorry, that's what Jessie and Sharise call her. I meant Monica… anyway, she knows more than what she has said." Tony was convinced that Monica was involved, but can't remember why or how. He was struggling and John could see it. They both just sat there for a few minutes. John finally broke the silence, "You asked if I would do something for you, what is it you have in mind?" Tony responded, "I need you to do something that you probably won't like very much." He then stopped and looked down at the floor for a moment. John said to him, "You know all you have to do is say the word and, as long as it's legal, it's done. You know that."

"I know John, and of course it's legal. I wouldn't ask you to do anything illegal. I don't want you and Becky to be cell mates you know. I don't trust you *that* much." Tony said with a chuckle. "I need you to check Monica out. I don't know why she keeps popping up, but she *has* to have something to do with it or she wouldn't keep coming up, right? I don't know how she is connected, just that she is. You gotta help me. Please John, please. I hate to say it, but my wife needs you." John just stared at him for a moment. Not quite sure how to answer him. "Are you saying you want me to investigate our best friend's wife? I need more to go on than a gut feeling. There needs to be a reason."

Tony rolled his chair back a little and turned around. He was starting to get very frustrated, he knew she was involved somehow, he also knew that if he was wrong Charles would never forgive him. He couldn't help his wife without finding out what caused his accident and the only way he could find that out was to find something to trigger his memory. The only thing he could remember was leaving the house and then waking up in the hospital. Everything in between was a blur. But *she* kept showing up in his mind. He turned back to John, "Something happened the night before the accident. Monica told Chucky that she didn't know where the little lady was. I know for a fact that she gave her permission to come over here, because I picked her up. She was there to see her off and then lied about it. She is constantly putting that little girl down and treats her worse than a slave. She creates issues that cause problems between Charles and Sharise. You can feel it when she walks in the room, she is pure evil. Even the kids know it. That's why they call her Demonica. And not just Jessie and Sharise, all the kids they hang out with know it and call her that. They see it, why can't Charles. We have tried to tell him, but he won't listen. I can't prove it, but I know she set up my Beck to take the fall for this. I just know it. I can *feel* it. I need something to show him, something that will make him see who she really is, not the loving, kind woman that he thinks she is, but the *real* her. The *evil* her. The one that shows up when he is not around."

John was completely taken aback by this request. "Tony," he said in a very calming voice, "you and I both know that what happened between you and her is not enough to show motive for attempted murder. She just caused a problem between a little girl and her father, nothing more. There is no reason to think that it was anything more than a misunderstanding or maybe a family feud. Nothing that would indicate she would be angry enough to try to kill you. I know you lost your memory, but now it seems like you have lost your senses too. I don't think that anything, outside of a true recovery of your memory, and your senses, will help her. Things are not going her way and I need to figure out something to help her. The only thing I can think of other than taking the plea bargain, which it is *very* clear neither of you want, is to take myself off the case to buy her some time. What you want me to do...what you are suggesting I do...it's crazy. That will only lead to pain." John turned to leave. Tony grabbed John's jacket. "please," he begged, "please…I know you think I am crazy, but please just check her out. If you find something on her, then it might help me remember. If not…. then you can have the true pleasure of saying I was wrong. If I am wrong, which I kinda hope I am, then Charles doesn't need to know anything about it, and there will be no harm done. But, if I'm right, then justice will have been served. I can't live without her John. She is my whole world. Her and Jessie are everything to me. Without her, I'm nothing. I love her more than life itself. She is the only thing that has kept me going since this happened." He said as he grabbed the arms of the chair then slapped his hands on them. "Without her, there is no sense in me going on. Jessie will have her mother and step dad, she won't need me anymore. I can't even hold her, read a bedtime story to her, or…" he stopped then fighting back the tears, he continued, "Jessie doesn't sleep most nights and the nights she does, she cries herself to sleep. Her grades have dropped, she wont even talk to me when she is here. She doesn't understand why she can't come back home full time, or why Becky isn't here when she does get to come home. I don't know what to tell her, she is so young to have been through everything she has been through so far. I don't know what to do to help her. Shoot, I can't even help myself." John stopped him. He was becoming very concerned about his friend. The way he is talking, he is worried about leaving him alone. "Tony, you are talking about basically killing yourself, then in the same breath, you say how concerned you are about what Jessie has been through in her young life. Could you really put her through more by taking her daddy away from her? Especially now?

I don't want to hear anymore of that kind of talk. You are scaring me, man. I will look into Monica. If you will make me a promise not to do anything stupid. I mean stupider than having me do a background investigation into one of our best friend's wife." Tony looked down at the floor for a moment, then back up to John, "I won't do anything stupid. I promise. Just please help Becky come home." John grabbed his hand and looked into his eyes, "I said I would look into her, and I will. One thing though, you have to keep the faith. We will get through this together. I will do everything I can. But you need to do something too, you need to rest, relax a little and remember. I will call you *if* I find something on Monica. If not…. well, let's just hope I can find something." John then turned and left.

After John left, Tony was really depressed. He went straight to bed. He had a difficult time falling to sleep. It wasn't enough that he had just accused his best friend's wife of attempted murder, but his braces were binding too. He had one of the nurses assist him in getting into bed and now he couldn't get to sleep. He couldn't get the events of the last few days off his mind. There was just something about Monica that he couldn't quite put his finger on. "Oh well," he thought, "tomorrow is a new day and the pain medication is finally taking effect." He finally drifted off to sleep.

It was 2:00 in the morning when he awoke in a cold sweat, his heart beating a mile a minute. He was disoriented and wasn't sure where he even was. Slowly his senses returned and he realized he was at home and that it was just a dream. After all, why would Monica stab him in the chest. If she wanted to kill him that bad, all she had to do was… "WAIT!!

That's it!!" he yelled out loud. Loud enough that the nurse that was staying in the room down the hall heard him. She was getting her robe on when she heard him yelling, "Marie?! Marie!! Get in here quick!!" she ran down the hall still putting on her robe as she entered the room. "Mr. Webster? Are you ok?" she said as she ran to his bed. "Never better!!" he said as he struggled to get out of the bed. "I need to get to the phone." Marie grabbed him as he was just about to fall out of the bed. "Mr. Webster, you do realize it is 2:00 in the morning? That's AM you know *after midnight* and *before* sunrise. Who do you think you are going to get to answer the phone at this time of the night? The only people who are up now are vampires and distraught nurses dealing with people like you. Now go back to sleep. I am sure what ever it is can wait until the sun comes up at least." Tony was not going to give in to her or any one else. "I said bring me the phone!! I know who tried to kill me. I have to warn Charles. She's crazed. She tried to kill me. I have to tell him now while I still remember!!" Now Marie's curiosity was getting the best of her. As she went to the other side of the room to get the phone, she asked, "Who's crazy and what does it have to do with Mr. Sloan?" she only knew Charles from his visits with Tony, but believed he was a good person. "Monica! Monica is crazy! If I don't warn Charles, he could be next! I have to tell Charles!"

Now she was just plain agitated, she placed the phone back down on the charger and shook her head, "Mr. Webster, Mr. Sloan is not going to want to hear this nonsense *after* sunrise, let alone in the middle of the night. Now please go back to sleep before I have to give you a sedative." She turned to walk out of the room.

Tony was getting very frustrated with her, "Fine! I'll just get the phone myself." Marie stopped and turned back to him, "Oh, and just how are you going to do that mister 'I can't get out of my bed by myself'? The phone is all the way over here and you are all the way over there. Now go back to sleep. I have had as much of this as I am going to tolerate for one night."

He knew he wasn't going to win this argument. She was right. He couldn't even get out of bed, let alone get across the room and get to the phone. And, even if he could, Charles is not going to want to hear this information during the day time, let alone in the middle of the night when he is half asleep. "Alright. Just make sure you are in here early. I don't want anything to happen to Charles and if I wait too long, he could be hurt, or even killed."

"I have to get the doctor to change his medication." She said in disgust as she left the room. He knew she didn't believe him, and that was fine, as long as Charles believes him, that's all that matters. He struggled to get back to sleep, but was still wide awake when Marie came in at 6:00.

"Are you awake? Do you still want to warn Charles or have you come to your senses?" Marie said as she brought his chair to his bed and set his robe on the bed. He knew he would not convince her, but he didn't have to. It was Charles that he would have to convince. That was a challenge he was not sure if he wanted to really face, but he knew he had to. "I told you last night, Marie, I know she is responsible for putting me into this chair. I don't want her to put Charles into a coffin. Now would you please bring me the phone."

Marie had no patience this morning for his nonsense. "You are one hard headed man, Mr. Webster, you know that right? I tell you what, let's get breakfast and get you dressed and then you can call anyone you want." She helped him get his robe on and get into his chair. As she walked away, she said, under her breath, "I don't know about this 'Monica' person, but I know *you're* crazy." She didn't realize he heard her. Tony really didn't care what she thought. He had finally remembered *everything* that happened and could not only save Charles, but get his wife back home. That's all he was concerned about… that and how he would explain to his best friend that the woman he just married was pure evil. "Do you know what this means, Marie?" he asked as he rolled out of the room. "It means that Becky will be home soon and Demonica will get what she deserves." Marie stopped and looked down at him, "Who is Demonica." Tony slipped up and knew it. "I meant Monica… just bring me the phone, please."

When Charles awoke that morning, he found a note by the coffee pot:

> *Charles,*
>
> *I have Sharise with me. When you come to your senses and divorce that evil thing you are married to, I will bring her back to you. I really hope you come back to us very soon, but until then, I will be protecting her the way you are not.*
>
> *I love you,*
>
> *Mom*

He couldn't believe it. His own mother has kidnapped his little angel. What was she thinking? "Monica!" he yelled "Monica wake up!! She's gone!!" he yelled again as he ran into the bedroom. "What...Who?... who's gone? What are you babbling about so early in the morning?" she mumbled as she sat up in the bed. Charles had already started getting dressed. "Sharise. Sharise is gone. Mom took her. She left me a note. I have to go get her." Monica moaned and dropped back down in the bed. "Now Charles, you know she is fine. Just calm down. Your mom is probably trying to help, in her own way. You know, since Tony's accident, you haven't exactly been yourself. All you can talk about is getting *Becky* out of jail." Charles couldn't believe what he was hearing, "That's not true. I talk about other things too." Monica rolled over on her side and said, "Oh yeah, like helping Tony get his memory back, finding a witness to the whole thing, which you will never do, oh, and spending almost all your waking hours either at Tony's or at the police station trying to 'help' them solve this case. You haven't been paying attention to either one of us. That's why your mom came to 'visit' in the first place. Your mom sees things clearer than you think. I can handle it, for a while, but Sharise really needs you. And, if you can't be there for her, then maybe she needs to be where someone can pay attention to her and care for her properly. She really can't understand at her age everything she has gone through in the past year. So, maybe, this is a good thing."

Charles calmed down a little bit. "Maybe you're right. I don't know that *I* understand it all. I guess right now she is better off with my mother. I'll call later and make sure they got home safely." He still didn't like the way Sharon just took her without saying anything to him, but maybe she is just trying to help. Charles finished getting dressed and headed back to the kitchen. Just as he was pouring his first cup of coffee, the phone rang. It was Tony. "What?... Really?... Great! I'll be there as soon as I can." He hung up the phone just as Monica was entering the room. "Great news!" he said, "Tony has regained his memory. I am headed there now." He walked passed her, gave her a kiss on the cheek and continued, "I'm not sure when I'll be back. If mom calls, tell her what happened and have her call me there." Monica appeared very surprised and almost frightened. She stood very still for a moment, then turned to him, "Charles..." she stopped. Charles turned around, "What?"

"Charles, I don't think that you should go to Tony right now." She said in a shaky voice. Charles was very confused. "Why? Did you not hear what I said? Tony regained his memory. He knows who did this to him and Becky. He needs me."

"Sharise needs you too. Don't you think you should go after her? I mean what right does your mother have to just take her like that? I think you should go after her first, then you can go talk to Tony. I mean he isn't going anywhere." she lightly chuckled, "Sharise needs you and she is your daughter." Charles was shocked by the sudden turn around. "What's the matter with you? You just said yourself that Sharise is in good hands. What's changed your mind? Nothing is going to happen to her. She is with people that love her and would never hurt her. Tony needs me right *now*. I can't turn my back on him. He's my best friend."

Monica sat down, and slowly looked up, she had regained her composure now, "But, you can turn your back on me. Is that it? I knew Tony would come first. Before me, before Sharise, before yourself even. How could you turn your back on the rest of us like that? Your own mother saw it and took your daughter because of it. Ever since the accident, all you ever talk about is how Tony needs you… or Becky needs you. No thought about how we need you. If you go now, I won't be here when you get back. I need to have someone that puts his family first, not back stabbing friends that try to put a wedge between you and the people that love you."

Charles walked back to the doorway to the kitchen. "What?! Monica, what are you going on about? You know that you and Sharise are my life. Tony is my best friend, but you, Sharise, my parents, you are my family. You would leave me because I'm trying to help a friend? What is going on, Monica? Why are you acting like this?" Monica dropped her head and started crying, "Monica, please tell me what is going on? What's wrong?" She sat there silent. Charles prodded her. "Please, tell me, what's got you so upset?"

She started talking slowly, "Charles, I…I can't let you go there. Don't you see?" He couldn't believe what he was hearing. "Why? What are you talking about?" He knelt down in front of the chair, lifted her head and looked into her eyes. "What has you so frightened that you want me to abandon Tony when he needs me? What is going on?" She turned away from him, "Don't you see, Charles? He's trying to hurt you. They staged the accident to try to tear us apart. They were angry when you and I got married. Don't you understand? Tony and Becky hate me and would do *anything* to get rid of me. I also think…no, you wouldn't believe me…"

"What?" he asked. "What wouldn't I believe?"

"Your mother. I think your mother is helping them. She never liked me either. I didn't think she would take Sharise, but that's got to be part of the plan. To make you choose between them, and me."

Charles stood up, shaking his head. She was right, he didn't believe her. No one would go to such lengths just to split up his marriage. No matter who he married. He *couldn't* believe it. But, he didn't want to lose Monica either. He thought a moment, "Darling, if you are that concerned, why don't you come with me? That way, if they are *luring* me into a trap you will be there to protect me." He said very sarcastically. She was not pleased with his tone, but maybe he was right. She could at least be there to hear what Tony has remembered. "Monica." He said harshly, "if you are coming with me, I am leaving now. Otherwise, stay here and wait for my mother to call."

Monica tried to be calm, even with the anger and fear boiling up inside her. "Charles, I think I would like to go, if you don't mind. I'm a little curious to see what triggered Tony's 'miraculous' memory restoration. I mean, let's face it, less than 24 hours ago, nothing. Now all of a sudden, total recall. It all sounds kinda fishy to me." Charles wasn't sure what was going on now, maybe after he talked to Tony, things would come together and make sense.

By the time they arrived at Tony's, John was already there. There was also another car that Charles did not recognize. They knocked on the door and it swung open seemingly by itself. They slowly walked in. Tony called out, "We're in here Chucky." They walked into the front room and found everyone standing around Tony. "I didn't know you were bringing *her*. Oh, well, it's probably just as well. I remembered what happened and I really don't think you are going to like it, Chuck. There is more to your wife than meets the eye."

Now, Charles is really confused. First Monica starts acting funny, then his best friend starts telling him that Monica is not who she seems. Exasperated, Charles shook his head and said, "Tony, please, just tell me what happened so I can go get Becky and we can get on with our life."

There was suddenly a very serious air about the room. All eyes turned to Tony. He hesitated as he was not sure how to continue without causing his best friend to be hurt any more than he has already been. He looked at his friend with concern. Then he turned his gaze to Monica. "Maybe you should ask her." Charles gave his friend a very confused look. "Why should I ask her? She was shopping at the time. She didn't even know about the accident until she got to the hospital. She wouldn't have any idea about what happened." Tony then looked over at Monica, she was very nervous and he could see it plainly in her eyes. He knew what she had done, and now he would have to try to force her to reveal it to everyone. Otherwise, he would have to try to explain it for her, and he knew there would be push back from Charles. "Oh, she knew about it all right, Chucky. She knew about it because she caused it. The only thing I don't know is why."

Monica suddenly got very defensive. "It's a Lie!!" she yelled. "Charles, darling, you can't possibly believe this, he is lying to save Becky. You don't believe it, do you? Please...I didn't do anything. He hates me. Everyone in your life hates me. I don't know why, but..."

Tony cut her off. "Monica, I never hated you. I have to admit, I never really liked you much, but I never hated you. The only thing I want to know is why?"

Monica started to back up. "No! I didn't do anything to you." She turned to her husband, "Charles, please, I told you before we left that they staged the accident to get me out of your life, now he's trying to pin it on me. He would do anything to keep his wife out of prison. You know that, Charles, everyone here knows that. He says he never hated me, but I know he's lying about that too. he hates me, Becky hates me, your mother, even Sharise who I have never done anything but love, hates me. Now they are trying to get rid of me and turn you against me. How could you possibly believe that I would do anything to harm him, or anyone else."

Tony looked at Charles, then back at Monica again, "Monica, stop. There is no reason to keep this up. I know what you did and how. I just haven't figured out the why. What did I do to make you want to kill me? Why did you go through all this trouble just to take me out?"

Charles was now very confused between her previous fear and why she didn't want him to come to talk to his best friend, could it be? "Monica? You were responsible for this? Why?"

"NO! You have no proof. Only the word of a paralyzed man who, until just a short time ago, had no recollection of the accident at all, and suddenly, regained his memory. You know that there is not a jury in the world that would convict me on that testimony alone. All I would have to do is point out the fact that his wife is facing a life sentence at the least, and the death penalty at the worst." She then turned to

Tony, "Everyone knows that your wife is the most important person in your life, and you would say anything to protect her. Even 'suddenly' remember something that you have no evidence of. I have nothing to worry about." Just then a stranger walked into the room. Tony looked up at him and then again at Monica. "Monica," he said, "I would like you to meet Edward. He is my first wife's new husband. He was there when you got into my car at Elsie's house. He saw you as plain as day. Elsie didn't see you, because she was in the house. But he did." He said as he nodded toward Edward. "He verified that part of my memory with John. Do you still want to deny it?"

Now Charles was dumbfounded. He couldn't believe that this was happening. "All right, let's just say that Monica did get in your car."

"She did." Edward interrupted.

"ok, she did." Charles acknowledged, "So why didn't you come forward earlier, Ed? Why now? What happened to suddenly bring you out of the wood work?"

"It's Edward," he clarified, "and I wasn't aware that there was any connection to the accident. Since Tony had no memory of what happened, or how, I didn't think it mattered. I didn't even know that Becky was in jail. Nobody told me. I guess because it had nothing to do with me directly. It wasn't until this morning, early, when John called, that I was even aware that there might be a connection. I thought it was truly an accident."

"Sorry, *Edward,*" Charles said rudely, "I didn't realize you weren't aware that Becky was in jail. I would think that your wife would talk to you about those kinds of important details. Or don't you two talk?"

"Careful, Chucky boy." Edward said, "you really don't want to upset me. My wife didn't know either. Tony kind of left that detail out." He looked down at Tony with annoyance. "Jessie never said a word either. I don't think she knows." Edward, being a bit larger than Charles, was kind of intimidating. "I don't blame him for not telling her, but he could have let us know. I would have said something."

Now Charles was getting very angry. "I don't believe you." He said, "I can't believe you stooped this low. How much did you have to pay this gargantuan to make up this crazy story? How much is Monica's life worth? I really need to know. How dare you! How dare you try to trade my wife's life for yours. I thought we were friends." He then turned to another he thought was his friend. "And John? Do you really believe this? Or maybe... was this your idea? I heard you would do anything to win a case, but I never would have thought you would go this far. Save your client at any cost, right? Even if it cost you a friendship and your soul." He paused for just a moment. "Did either of you even consider the facts. The wig and the opium were not found in my wife's possession, but in Becky's. My wife has witnesses to her whereabouts, Becky does not. My wife has no reason to want Tony dead. What about those facts? What about that truth?"

Tony couldn't believe what he was hearing. "And what reason would my wife have Charles? Why would she want me dead? What possible reason? Tell me that Chucky. Answer that question, will you?"

"It's *Charles*." He said. "and that is an easy one. Money. If you die, she stands to inherit everything, since Elsie is now remarried, not to mention your life insurance." Tony started laughing.

"What's so funny?" Charles did not see any humor in this whole thing. "Please share the joke with the rest of us. God knows we all could use a good laugh."

"Oh, Chucky. Becky doesn't get any money. Well, not much anyway. Just enough to live on. The rest goes into a trust for Jessie, and you, by the way Charles, are the trustee and executer. And as far as life insurance, there's just enough to bury me. And that goes directly to the mortuary. So, you see, there goes your whole theory and the basis for my loving Beck to want me dead. I am worth more to her alive."

John spoke up, "So much for the money theory. Now what Charles? What's her other motive?"

Now Charles wasn't sure what to believe. Could the woman he loves be so heartless? Could she possibly have been behind this whole thing? No, it's not possible. "O.K. so let's say that what you said is true. Let's say she did get into the car with you, what does that prove? What is *her* motive? Why would she want you dead?"

Tony looked over at Monica, "Why don't you answer that one Monica? Or do you even know why you did this?" Monica had a look of fear in her eyes as she stammered, "I…I… I don't know what you are talking about." She had now regained her composure, "I was never at Elsie's house. I don't even go into that part of town." Charles looked a little puzzled as she continued, "They don't have any decent shopping or any other reason to go there. The only buildings they even have are a few small houses. Not my ideal destination." She said smugly.

Charles paused a few minutes. Tony recognized the look on his face. It was the same as when he was finally coming to the realization that Jamie was truly gone and never coming back. It was a look of shock, disbelief, and anxiety. He turned away from everyone. He was having a hard time believing that this is actually happening. He just stood there, trying to find the right words to say. He just couldn't believe it was true. He knew he had never told her where Elsie lived, because he didn't know himself. He wasn't sure how to say that without actually sounding accusing himself. He wants so much to believe that Monica is innocent. How can make everyone believe that his loving wife could not possibly have had anything to do with this, when he is not sure himself. He couldn't. There is no possible way she could have known where Tony was going. Unless….unless she followed him? No. She was shopping with friends, no where near where Tony was. As he stood there thinking, he hadn't heard what was going on in the conversation behind him. Tony asked him, "Charles…? Did you even hear what I said?" Charles turned back to the rest of the people in the room. "Huh…what? Sorry I was thinking." Tony continued, "I was just asking Monica how she knew where Elsie lives. I know I didn't tell her, and, as far as I know you don't know where she lives. I was trying to clarify that with you. But, you seemed to be on another planet. Or at least another zone. Would you like to clarify for me whether or not you know where my ex-wife lives?"

Charles hesitated a moment. "I don't know where she lives." He said quietly. John reached over and grabbed his shoulder gently, "Please speak up, Charles." Charles dropped his head and said in a louder voice, "I don't know where she lives. I don't know what part of town. I don't know how she knows, but apparently from her statement, she knows." He was still not convinced that Monica was guilty, but he wasn't convinced she was innocent either. He looked at her with pleading eyes. "Monica, how did you know where Tony was? Why were you there? Who told you even where Elsie and Edward live?"

Monica knew she had made a mistake and she would have to come up with something quickly to cover it up. She thought a moment, "Becky told me." She said, "She said if anything happened to her or Tony, I was to take Jessie to her mothers house and gave me the address. I drove over there a few weeks ago to make sure I could find the place just in case. It is not a bad neighborhood, just not one that I would be in unless I had to. Charles, you believe me, don't you? I don't know what I would do if I thought you believed I could do something that would hurt anyone. I am not that kind of person." So now Charles turned to John, "John, I think we need to find a way to settle this without any unnecessary arrests. If you can convince me that there is any *real* evidence to show motive, means, and opportunity, then I will take her to jail myself. I won't even wait for Lloyd to get here. But I do require actual evidence, not hearsay. If you can't provide me with that, then you need to find another way to defend your client."

Monica was relieved. At least Charles believed her. He was the only one who did. "Darling," she said as she turned to leave, "I have had quite enough of this. I wish to go home now." Charles was not ready to leave. "I think we need to stay for a while," he said, "I need to be clear on exactly what happened. So far, we have only heard part of the story, just that you may or may not have been in the car with Tony at the time of, or just before the accident. I think we need to hear the rest. Don't you?"

Monica did not want to hear the rest. She wanted to forget the whole thing. "I really don't want to hear any more lies. I have had enough for one day. Actually, I have had enough for a lifetime. There is no reason to continue this absurdity. As if I am capable of kidnapping anyone, let alone killing someone. Not likely." Now everyone stared at Monica. John tried to slowly leave the room when Tony looked over at him, he suddenly stopped. "John?" Tony asked, "Are you going somewhere?" "No." John responded. "I was just trying to get a little more comfortable." Tony looked back at Monica. "Monica? What are you talking about? Nobody ever said anything about kidnapping anyone, and although I was in a horrible accident, I am very much alive and plan on staying that way." Monica now started backing up. She was almost to the doorway when Charles stopped her. "Monica, please answer the question, who was kidnapped? Who said anything about killing anyone?" She wasn't sure how to answer. He was right, she had once again slipped up. She only knew that she needed to leave. "Charles, darling, they were insinuating that I kidnapped Tony and tried to kill him, that was all I was referring to." She said nervously. "You know me, you know I could never hurt anyone. I…I don't understand why you are making me stay and listen to this garbage. Please, I just want to go home…please."

Now John was also starting to act a little nervous. "Charles, maybe you should just take her home. We don't really have any evidence. So, you can just take her home." He said as he looked at Monica with a look of panic. "She…she just needs to rest. Maybe we all do. I…" Tony interrupted. "Rest? You think that she needs to rest? My wife is not resting. She is sitting in a jail cell afraid for her life. You are supposed to be defending *her* not the one that is actually guilty. I remember her in the car with me. I remember we stopped to get a cup of coffee. She told me she was concerned about Sharise. She said that Charles was angry because she told him that I didn't pick the little lady up and that she was lying to him. I also remember her saying she would catch a cab instead of letting me take her home, even though I was already going there. She said she had something to take care of and would be there when she was done. The next thing I know I am drifting off and woke up upside down in the car. When the ambulance got there, they strapped me to a back board and took me to the hospital. I woke up alone, begging for someone to get my wife. You all know the rest." Just at that moment, Jessie came out of her room. "Daddy? What's going on?" Tony looked over at her. "Baby, just go back to your room. It's all ok." Jessie knew that whatever was happening out here was much more exciting than what was going on in her room. "But, Daddy…" Monica walked over to her, bent down to her level and, speaking in a tone that she thought no one else could here spoke to the child "Look you little monster, this is big people talk and you need to get out! No brats allowed." Jessie almost started to cry. Her lower lip quivered. Charles was stunned "Monica!!! What has gotten into you? How dare you talk to her like that?" As Monica looked around, she realized that everyone had heard her. She said, "I'm sorry, you're right. I am just a little tense.

I have never been accused of such crimes before in my life. I just don't know how to act."

Charles sat down in the chair behind him, head in his hands, not sure what to think. He began to cry himself. Not since his beloved Jamie died, has he felt so out of control. John walked up to him and put his hand on his shoulder. "Charles?" Charles looked up at him tears still streaming down his face. "John, I just don't know what to believe. I need a drink." John shook his head, "It's a bit too early in the day for a drink, pal. Besides, we all need to keep a clear head." Charles took a deep breath and wiped the tears from his eyes, "You're right, John. I just don't know…"

Tony interrupted again, "Hey guys, why don't we just ask Jessie and Sharise what's been going on." Tony just realized that Sharise wasn't there. "Where is the little lady Charles?" Charles, still trying to completely regain his composure, said, "She's at my mom's house. Apparently, as usual, mom thinks she knows best and took her home with her this morning." Charles then looked over at Jessie. "Jessica? I need you to tell me the absolute truth. Do you understand me?" Jessie nodded. "I need to know exactly why you think that Monica is so mean to you. What did she do or say to you and Sharise that made you think she is so evil?" Monica stepped between the two of them, "Surely you are not going to take the word of a child over mine. You know they make things up to keep themselves out of trouble." Charles held his hand up to Monica as if to shut her up, then motioned his hand to make it very clear as he closed the tips of his fingers to his thumb telling her to stop talking. Monica then stepped aside as if she were a wounded dog. "Jessica," Charles continued, "you know we love you very much and whatever you tell us,

as long as it is the truth, will not make us angry with you."
Jessie knew that uncle Charles was already very upset. He
very rarely called her "Jessica" unless something was wrong
or she was in trouble. She nodded her head in response. She
still didn't know exactly what to say, because she was still
afraid that uncle Charles would be upset. He said he loves
Demonica and, even though she didn't understand why, she
knew that he would not like to hear the truth. It is going to
hurt him and she really didn't want that. Uncle Charles was
her best adult friend and didn't want him to go through the
same thing he went through when Sharise lost her mommy.
She paused, just for a moment. "Uncle Charles, if I tell you
the truth, you can't be mad at me. I don't want you to cry
again." He looked at her very sternly, "Jessie, I need you to
tell me the truth. What happened to you and my baby girl?"
Jessie climbed into her daddy's lap and dropped her head.
"You're not going to believe me." Tony wrapped his arms
around her as best he could. "Honey, we will believe you
as long as you promise it is the truth." She looked up at her
daddy and then to Charles. "Daddy, she hates us. She…"
Jessie stopped. Tony urged her. "It's ok honey, go on. No
one is going to hurt you" Jessie continued, "She will." She
said as she pointed to Monica. "She said if we told any body
what she did, she would do the same thing to us that she did
to Shari's mommy. She would hurt us bad or kill us and no
one would know it was her. Just like Shari's mommy. She
killed her." Jessie started to cry again. Then she continued,
"She said this time no one would even find the bodies." She
stopped again not knowing what to say next. "Daddy, please
don't let her hurt me!! Please!! I want to see Sharise I want
her to be ok!!" Tony and Charles were both stunned as they

looked over at Monica. She had a blank expression. Now she wasn't sure what to say.

Charles asked Tony, "You got your phone handy?" Tony reached down on the handle of his wheelchair, "Of course, I always have it. I had it built into the chair, why?"

"I need to talk to Sharise. Would you call my mom's house?"

"Sure, Charles. Give me just a minute and I will have her on speaker phone." Tony said as he dialed the number.

Sharon had just finished the dishes from a late breakfast when the phone rang. "Hello," she said. "Mom, I need to talk to Sharise." Charles said very curtly. "Charles?... first off you don't talk like that to me. Secondly, Sharise isn't here. She was still asleep when I left your house this morning, at least, I think she was. I didn't go into her room. It was very early and I didn't want to risk waking her up. She's been through quite enough and needs her rest. I went out and locked the door behind me. What's going on son? Why would you think she is with me?" Charles looked over at Monica. She just shook her head, "No, Charles, no. I didn't do anything to her. I didn't hurt the little b... baby. They are making this up. Those little brats are trying to get rid of me."

Charles, still looking at Monica, now with a bit of concern, answered his mother, "I'm not sure what is going on, but there was a note next to the coffee pot this morning that said you took her with you…I need to go now. I think there is something I need to discuss with my wife." He hung up and started toward Monica. "Where is my daughter? What did you do?"

Monica started to back up slowly toward the front door she had a look of fear and was almost at tears as she said, "I didn't do anything. I don't…I don't know where she is. I…"

She then turned and ran out of the house, jumped into Tony's new car and drove off tires screeching, smoke pouring from them.

As Tony held her, jessie started crying again. "I told you daddy. I told you she is evil. She talks that way to me and Sharise all the time. She is mean!!" She started crying even harder. Tony, trying to comfort her softly said, "My little angel. I am so sorry I didn't believe you. I thought she was just being more strict than you were used to. I really didn't know what she was doing to you and Sharise. Please forgive me."

Meanwhile, Charles got into his own car and started after Monica. She was driving like a maniac when he finally caught up to her, he motioned for her to pull over, she looked at him with tears in her eyes and shook her head. Taking her eyes off the road just for that short period of time was enough. She didn't see the upcoming turn until it was too late. She slammed on the brakes, but was unable to maintain control. The vehicle spun around a full 360 degrees then went flying off the road coming to a very sudden stop at the bottom of a ravine. Charles slammed

on his brakes. He was going as fast as she was, but was able
to maintain control and get the car stopped just before the
edge of the road. He jumped out and ran to her, reliving
the horror of Jamie's accident as he slid down the ravine to
the car. "Jamie!? Jamie, say something please!" He heard a
low moan. She was alive! It was just then that he realized
that he had actually called her Jamie instead of Monica.
He couldn't believe after all this time, he still wasn't over
his beloved Jamie's death. He called Lloyd and told him
where they were. He struggled to open the door of the car.
The impact of the crash was enough to cause the front of
the vehicle to be forced back crushing the hinges and latch
of the door and shattering the window. He kept jerking on
the door handle. He couldn't get it to open. He reached
in through the opening where the window had been, and
grabbed the inside handle of the vehicle, cutting his arm on
the glass that was left over from the window. He continued
to struggle to open the door. Being unsuccessful, he rushed
to the passenger side of the vehicle. The damage was not
as severe on that side. After a few moments of struggling,
he was able to force the door open. He crawled through
to her. She was lying very still, but breathing. "Monica,
I'm sorry." He said softly, feeling a little guilty as if he had
caused this. After all, if he hadn't taken her attention off the
road, maybe she wouldn't be lying in a ravine, holding on
for dear life. He just sat there staring at the floor of the car,
not knowing what to say. Monica moaned and he turned
his gaze to her. He reached over and grasped her hand. It
was limp and cold. He was suddenly very frightened, not
so much at the potential of losing his new wife as she had
proven she didn't truly love him, but that he may never find

out where his daughter is. He leaned over and whispered to her, "Monica, if you can hear me, please," he begged, "please tell me where my little girl is. I can forgive a lot, but if she is hurt, I don't think I could forgive myself, let alone you." Monica opened her eyes just a little, it was obviously difficult for her, "I...I..." just then, she passed out again. He started to sob. He continued to hold onto her cold hand until the ambulance arrived. They had to cut her out of the vehicle. Since there was special equipment added to allow for Tony to drive the vehicle, it was especially difficult. Once they were able to get to her, they gently slid a backboard underneath her, braced her neck and carefully pulled her from the wreckage. They loaded her into the ambulance and left for the hospital. Lloyd had arrived at the same time as the ambulance and quickly stopped Charles as he was headed to his car to follow. "Hold on there. I need to know what happened here before you go anywhere." Charles grabbed Lloyd's hand and removed it from his arm. "Lloyd, she knows where my baby girl is, she is the only one that knows. You are not going to stop me. I have to find her." Lloyd, not having been informed of Sharise's disappearance, was very confused. "Wait...what? What are you talking about? What's happened to Sharise?" Lloyd was as close to Charles as anyone, and considered Sharise as his own niece. He grabbed Charles again, this time by the shoulder, and a little more gently "You need to stop and tell me what is going on." Charles was not about to stop for any reason, he was not about to let his daughter spend another minute away from him than absolutely necessary. "Lloyd, I don't know what exactly is going on. All I know is that my little girl is not where I thought she was, Monica knows where she is, and *I* have to find her. I really wish I had more to tell you, but that is all I am certain of. Now please," He said as he reached for Lloyds hand, still on his shoulder, "please, let me go find my baby girl." Lloyd refused to let go. He pulled Charles around where he could face him. "I have no idea what you are talking about, but it is *my* job to find out, not yours. You are, once again, not in any condition to drive yourself anywhere. Let me take you to the hospital. As soon as we can, we will talk to her and get to the bottom of this. In the meantime, you need to calm down and let me do my job." Charles was beginning to get furious. "Your job!!?? Your job!!??" he yelled, "You couldn't find out what happened to my Jamie!!! Why would I trust you to find out what has happened to my baby girl!!?? Maybe you didn't hear me, she is missing and I don't know how long she has been gone. I don't know where she is, I don't know if she is hurt or…. or…worse." He stopped talking and started sobbing. Lloyd reached out and grabbed both shoulders, pulling him toward him, he allowed Charles to continue sobbing. He grabbed Lloyd and held on as if he would never let go. Lloyd held his friend, knowing that there was nothing he could do to stop his pain except find his little girl. He knew that what Charles had just said was said in pain, not true anger. Having himself gone through the loss of his own family. After a few minutes, Charles stopped crying and lifted his head, pushed away from Lloyd and put his head down. He knew what he said was not true. Lloyd had done everything he could to find out exactly what happened to Jamie, he actually went above and beyond to try to find something. He looked up and said quietly, "I'm sorry. I don't know what got into me. I just feel so helpless, I…" His

Friend stopped him, "I know. Don't worry about it. Let's go find out where that little lady of yours is. I'm sure she is fine. If Monica had anything to do with her disappearance, she will pay. I promise you that." The two of them got into Lloyd's patrol car and headed to the hospital. When they arrived, Charles rushed through the emergency room doors and up to the nurse's station. "Can I help you?" the nurse asked. "Yes, my wife, Jamie…I mean Monica just came in by ambulance. She was in an accident. I need to speak to her." The nurse gave him a look of disgust. "It sounds like you have too many wives, sir. In any case, I will need her full name, whichever one it is that is here." Charles shook his head. "I only have one wife, my first wife died…any way I need to talk to my wife Monica Sloan. She was just brought in by…" the nurse interrupted him, "I heard the first time, she was in an accident. What is your first name?"

"My name is Charles, Charles Sloan. I need to talk to my wife immediately before it's too late. You don't understand."

"Mr. Sloan," she said calmly, "I understand you want to talk to your wife but I can't take you back to talk to her until I find her and find out if she is able and willing to talk to you. So have a seat and we will call you when you can come back." Charles started to say something back to her when Lloyd stepped between him and the nurse's desk. "Charles, go sit down while I talk to this young lady." He then turned to the nurse as Charles headed into the waiting area to sit down. "Miss, I know that you are just doing your job," he said, "but, I also have a job to do. There is a little girl out there somewhere that may be in trouble. This man's wife may be the only one that knows where she is. We need your help. So, if you would please, go find Mrs. Sloan so we can talk to her before something happens that all of us are going to be very upset about. Do you think you can do that? Please?" The nurse glared at him. "I don't like being talked to that way." She said as she stood up and walked back to the examination rooms. Lloyd went over and sat next to his friend, "I think I won her over." He said snidely. Charles chuckled lightly and shook his head. As they sat there, waiting neither of them really knew what to say to the other. They couldn't believe what had just transpired in the last few hours. Suddenly Charles realized that he had not let anyone else know that Monica had been hurt, not that they would care about her, but the fact that she may be the only one that knows where his little girl is, may be of concern. He reached for his phone just as it started to ring. "Hello?" It was Sharon, "Charles? Are you there?" Charles answered her, "Yes, mom, I am here." "What is going on, Charles? I have been trying to reach you and you haven't been answering. Where are you, and where is Sharise?" Charles paused, not sure how to answer her, he still wasn't exactly sure what had happened. "Mom...I...I'm at the hospital. Monica was in an accident." Sharon didn't even try to hide her feelings this time, "I hope she's in pain." "Mom!! Please!! She took Sharise. She's the only one that knows where she is." "WHAT!! What do you mean she *took* her? Where? Why? She better not have hurt my angel. I will take her out myself." Charles didn't even try to calm her down, he knew it would not do any good anyway. "Mom, I don't know the wheres or whys just that she took her. I am trying to find out now, but they are not telling us anything yet. The nurse went back a few minutes ago, as soon as we know I will let you know." "We?" she asked, "who is we?"

"Lloyd is here with me, mom. He is trying to move things along a little."

"Good, maybe he can get her to talk by, oh, I don't know, yanking her fingernails out, or waterboarding, something gentle like that."

"You know, sometimes I really can't believe that you are my mother. Seriously." He said as he shook his head. "I'm glad Lloyd couldn't hear you on that one."

"You're right. I shouldn't say things like that. You know I don't mean it. I will be heading that way this afternoon. I know you don't want me there, but I am coming anyway. I love you, son."

"I love you too mom. See you soon."

After he hung up with her Charles called Tony. "Hello," Tony said. "Hey Tony" Charles answered, "Monica was in an accident in your car. She is seriously injured. Lloyd is here with me. We are waiting to hear something about her condition, but they won't let me back to see her yet."

"Chuck, I am so sorry. Has she said anything at all?"

"No. Nothing. She was unconscious at the scene, and as far as I know, still is." Just then the nurse came back out. "Mr. Sloan?"

"Tony, I gotta go, the nurse just called. I'll call you back."

"Chuck…" Tony was cut off when Charles hung up. He stood up and walked to where the nurse was. "Your wife is in surgery. The doctor will be out as soon as they are done to let you know how it went." Charles was stunned, "It took you this long to come out to tell me this? Did you not hear what he said when we came in?" he asked as he pointed to Lloyd. "The little girl he spoke to you about, she is my daughter.

That woman in there is most likely the only one…" "I know," she interrupted, "the only one that knows where she is. I heard. If you want to talk to her, you will have to wait until she is out of recovery. It may be quite a while; can I get you something to drink or a magazine?" Charles was about to lose it when once again his friend saved him from losing his temper completely. "A cup of coffee would be great, thank you." Lloyd said to the nurse. He then grabbed Charles' arm and led him back to the chair he was sitting in. "Look, you can't talk to her right now, but you can talk to Tony. Why don't you call him back, since you hung up on him, and find out what he was trying to tell you. Maybe he knows something, maybe he remembered her saying something or doing something that might tell us where our little girl is." Charles slumped down in the seat, "I don't know, I just don't think she would have told him anything." Lloyd nodded in agreement. So, they sat there, drinking the coffee that the nurse brought them, and waited. Pretty soon, Lloyd got up and walked to the other side of the room. Charles could see him making a call, but could not hear what he was saying. After several minutes, he hung up and made a second call. Charles realized that he was trying to get more information on Monica. Where she might have been, where she might have taken Sharise, what she might have done to her. He could only imagine what his little girl was going through. He was afraid he might never see her beautiful blue eyes again. Why could he not see the same things that everyone else apparently saw in the woman he was so captivated by? What had he done to his precious little angel? She tried to tell him. His mother tried to tell him. Even Tony tried to warn him, but he wouldn't listen. Now, he had to face the fact that he was wrong. Even worse, his baby girl is paying the price. What she must be going through. She must be scared to death. Alone, anxious, feeling abandoned? Like he doesn't love her? What was he thinking, marrying another woman so soon without knowing enough about her, without *really* knowing her at all? He sat there thinking about all the things he wants to tell his little angel, how he was wrong, how it will never happen again, if only he knew where she was. "Oh, God!" he cried, he looked around he realized he had said it out loud. Lloyd heard him, cut his last call short, and came running to his friend. "Charles? What is it? What's wrong?" Charles just sat there with his head in his hands. He was so overcome with fear he couldn't speak, just thinking about what his daughter must be going through. He was not even aware that Lloyd had come back until he reached out and touched his back. Charles jumped out of his seat, fists clenched, then suddenly realized it was his friend trying to comfort him. "Sorry, I didn't mean to startle you. I called Tony. John left his house suddenly just after you went after Monica. He was trying to tell you that when you hung up on him earlier. So, I made a few additional calls. Charles? Charles are you listening to me...can you even hear me." Charles had started to zone out again. "Charles!? HEY!! CHUCK!!" still no response. Lloyd called the nurse over, he was very concerned about his friend. He had never seen him like this before. Not even after Jamie was killed. He had seen him in shock, but not like this. The nurse came over, looked at Lloyd and slapped Charles as hard as she could in the face. Charles, again startled yelled, "What did you do that for!?" She shook her head, "You were in a daze, you needed a little 'jolt' to bring you back to reality. Your friend is trying to tell you something." She looked at Lloyd, "You're a cop, right? You should have known how to handle that one." She then turned to walk away, stopped, turned back around and said with a smile, "no charge." Then turned again and walked back to her desk. They both stood there for a moment, still a little taken aback. Then Lloyd looked back at Charles, "as I was saying, John left Tony's house quite suddenly just after you left to chase down your wife so, I made a few other phone calls to check on something." Charles looked puzzled "what? What about John?" Lloyd was now becoming a little frustrated. "Look, Charles, John is involved. He knew Monica before."

"What are you talking about Lloyd, how could John know her?"

Lloyd continued, "Do you remember the story he told about his brother? How he went to prison and was killed after being wrongfully convicted of assault?"

"Yeah, what about it?"

"Well, the woman that was involved, the wife of the man that was actually guilty of the crime, that was Monica's mother. As it turns out, the man that was assaulted wasn't the only one having an affair with her. Tom, Johns brother, was also involved with her. As a matter of fact, there is some doubt about who Monica's biological father was, or is. The man that raised her may not have been her true father. There are rumors that *Tom* may have actually been her biological father. John found that out and went looking for her. a few years later, he apparently found her, in a not so healthy lifestyle." Charles looked completely confused, "What are you saying, Lloyd?" Lloyd continued, "Apparently, Monica was working for the one of the largest drug cartels in the

U.S. Her boss, who was also her husband, was in a lot of trouble, and she convinced John that Tom *was* her father and that since she was a blood relative, he had no choice but to help her out and become her husbands defense attorney. John agreed, and started working for him on retainer. At one point her husband was charged with murder, a murder that John knew he had ordered. John refused to defend him on that charge and was told that if he did not defend him, he himself would be 'given up' as the guilty party. John still refused, there was an 'altercation' and Monica's husband was killed. Monica was the only witness. She promised him she would keep her mouth shut as long as he made sure that she would be taken care of in the same way that she had become accustomed to." Lloyd stopped to take a drink of his, now cold, coffee. He shuttered, "yuck, that is nasty when it's cold." Charles prodded him, "Lloyd, you were saying?" Lloyd finished his horrible, cold coffee, then continued, "That's it." Charles grabbed his friend's arm, "What? What do you mean 'that's it'? That cant be all there is. What does that have to do with what happened to my daughter? How does that help her?"

Now Lloyd really wasn't sure what to say, he really didn't know any more than that. "I guess, we need to find John to find out what it has to do with you and Sharise. And, hopefully, he knows where to find our angel." He said as he tossed the paper coffee cup into the trash next to him. He started heading to the exit, turned back to Charles, "you comin?" Charles rushed to catch up to him. "Where do we start?" he asked. As they were just about to the door, the nurse hollered out, "Mr. Sloan. Mr. Sloan?" Charles turned and went back to the desk. "Yes." He said. "Your wife is out of surgery and in recovery, you can go back and sit with her if you would like." He looked at her with a very strange look, as though he were expecting more. There was an awkward silence. He finally asked her, "can she talk yet?" the nurse answered him slowly, "no…she can't talk yet. But she would probably like to have her husband next to her when she wakes up." Charles just shook his head, "I really doubt that. I don't think she is going to want to see me at all. And frankly, unless she can talk to me, I don't want to be anywhere near her. But, thank you anyway." He then headed back to where Lloyd was waiting, leaving the nurse scratching her head and completely confused.

As they got into the patrol car, Lloyd asked, "Do you know where John lives?" Charles answered as he stopped putting his seatbelt on, "Yep, sure do. Want me to drive?" "Nope. Just point the way Rudolph." Lloyd answered, referring to his favorite bird dog Charles finished putting on his seatbelt, "Rudolph…really? Now I'm a dog?" Lloyd just chuckled as he started the car. "It's a compliment. He's never steered me wrong."

As they headed to Johns house, lights flashing, siren blaring, Charles guiding the way, they were both hoping and praying that John knew where Sharise was. As they got closer, Charles started to tell Lloyd to shut off the lights and siren, just as Lloyd reached over to do that very thing. As they turned the corner to start down the street that John lived on, they both saw him loading something in his car.

John looked up, saw them coming up the road, and rushed into the house, leaving the item that he was starting to load half in and half out of the trunk. Almost before the vehicle stopped, Charles jumped out and followed him into the house. Lloyd put the car in park and rushed in behind him. As he ran into the house, he saw Charles, John in his grasp, getting ready to hit him square in the mouth. "Charles!" Lloyd yelled. Charles stopped mid strike, not taking his eyes off of John, and yelled back, "What! He has my little girl! He's going to tell me where she is and why he took her!" Lloyd grabbed his fist, "He won't be able to tell you anything if you break his jaw. Think about what you are doing, for once." Lloyd was not letting him hurt their last chance to find Sharise. Charles released him and John fell to the ground. He crawled into the corner of the room. Lloyd then looked at John, cowering against the wall, so terrified that he could barely move. "Get up, you pathetic excuse of a man." John shook his head. "No. I get up, he's gonna knock me down." He said as he nodded toward Charles. Lloyd looked at Charles, who still hasn't taken his eyes off John, "Charles? No, you don't have to worry about him, he wants to know what you did with his little girl. If he knocks you down, you won't be able to talk, so, I won't be able to ask you nicely where she is." John remained where he was, shaking his head, not taking his eyes off of Charles. Suddenly, they heard something. It sounded like a moan. John started crawling toward the basement door. Charles glared at him as if he were burning a hole in his heart. Lloyd reached down and grabbed John by the arm, turned him around and put handcuffs on him. He then set him down in a nearby chair. "You move, and I will not stop him from breaking any bone he chooses. You understand me? You were supposed to be his friend. You need to tell us where she is." Just then they heard the moan again, it seemed to be coming from the vent in the floor. "Is that her!?" Charles demanded as he grabbed his former friend by the arm. "you better not have hurt her!!" John cowered again afraid that he was about to be struck by a man that he still, even now, believed was his friend. "She's fine, Charles. I would never have hurt her. She is in the basement bedroom. The key is on the top of the fridge." He said, his voice matching the trembling of the rest of his body. "Please, Charles, Lloyd, you have to believe I would never hurt her. She's like my own daughter. I couldn't hurt her." Charles rushed to the kitchen, reached up onto the refrigerator, and after feeling around for a few moments, found the key. He then ran down the stairs to the only bedroom in the basement with a closed door. He fumbled with the key, so eager to get his baby back, he dropped it. Not just once, but twice. He stopped took a deep breath, picked up the key, and calmly unlocked the door. What he saw inside the room surprised him. He wasn't sure what he really expected to find, but it certainly wasn't this. The room was painted pink with puppies and rainbows. The twin sized bed centered in the room had two matching nightstands, it was a very cheerful, comforting room. It was then that he realized there was a body lying in the bed. His heart stopped, he was terrified that it was his little girl, and also that it wasn't. He slowly entered the room, cautious, anxious. He carefully reached for the blanket suddenly Sharise leapt out of the bed, scaring Charles so badly that he fell backward crashing into a toybox and knocking over a small child sized table that had been set up for a "tea party".

She ran over to him, "Daddy!?" she squealed. "Daddy! what are you doing here? Monica and Uncle John said you were goin way with *her* again." Charles could not believe his eyes or ears, his baby girl was not only ok, but had no idea that she had even been kidnapped in the first place. She jumped into his arms. "I'm glad you didn't go." Charles hugged his little angel so tightly that she tapped him on the shoulder, "Daddy, I can't breathe." He released his tight hug and once again there were tears in his eyes, this time they were tears of joy. "What say we get outta here." He said, as if nothing were wrong. "Ok." She said. "But I need to find uncle John and let him know your back." "He knows, my sweet little angel, he knows."

As they walked back up the stairs Sharise was telling her daddy how much fun she had with 'uncle john'. "He played 'tea party' with me, we went out for ice cream, even though it was kinda early, he said it was a special cassion. Then his phone rang and he had to go, so he told me to stay in the room downstairs cause he wanted me to be safe, and couldn't take me with him. He even put pizza and soda in the room for me case I got hungry or thirsty. Can I do this again daddy?" Charles wasn't sure how to break the news that she was not going to see 'uncle John' again. As they were headed out the front door, she saw one of Lloyd's deputies helping John into his car. She looked up at her daddy, the look on his face was a look she had seen before and she knew not to ask him questions when he looked like that. Then she looked over and saw Lloyd, "Uncle Lloyd!" she squealed again as she ran over to him. He knelt down allowing her to wrap her arms around his neck and then rose with her in his arms. He walked over to his friend, put his arm around his shoulder and said, "come on, I'll give you a ride back to your car." Charles, suddenly realized that his mother was supposed to meet him at the hospital. "Lloyd? Would you mind taking me back to Monica?" Sharise's glee suddenly turned to anger. She still didn't like her. "Daddy, can I just stay with uncle Lloyd, or maybe he could take me to uncle Tony's" Charles reached over Lloyds shoulder and patted her on the head, "No, Sharise, Monica is in the hospital. We are going to meet your grandma there and let them both know that you have been found safe and sound." Now Sharise was really confused. "Found? I didn't know I was lost." Charles smiled and ruffled her hair. She usually didn't like it, but for some reason, this time was ok. Lloyd loaded his precious cargo into the back seat of his patrol car, then got into the passenger seat. Charles looked at him once again confused. "Lloyd...you got into the wrong seat." Lloyd looked back at Sharise gave her a smile and a wink. Then looked straight ahead "Nope, you're driving. You earned it." He said to Charles as he put his seatbelt on. "You can even turn on the lights and siren. He winked at Sharise again. "Please, daddy, can I turn on the siren?" As Charles climbed into the driver's side, he looked back at her, smiled and said, "Angel, I would let you do that, but you don't have long enough arms to reach the front seat." He, too, winked at her, reached over and turned on the lights and siren and headed to the hospital. This was so much fun Sharise didn't even mind the fact that she had to see Demonica again. Besides gramma was going to be there too. As they pulled into the hospital, once again, they entered through the emergency room doors and walked up to the nurse's station. The same nurse was there. When she looked up and saw them, again, she shook her head in disbelief. She mumbled, sarcastically, under her breath, "how did I get so lucky twice in one day?" Charles heard her, but he really didn't care. He was almost as happy right now as he was when Sharise was born. He looked her right in the eye and said with a smile, "You just must be the luckiest woman in the world." She chuckled a little. "Are you finally ready to see your wife? She's been asking for you. I don't know what she did, but she has been saying she's sorry for the last 30 minutes. You might want to forgive her." Charles shook his head, "No Ma'am, no forgiveness here. She has lost that option." Now Sharise was really confused. First her daddy says he has to tell Demonica he found her safe and sound, then he talks like that? Suddenly, she remembered her grandma was supposed to be there too. "Daddy, where's Gramma?" just at that moment, as if by magic, Sharon walked in the door. Charles stopped for a moment then turned around. "Mom, I am so happy to see you." He walked over to her and gave her a big hug. "Come on, let's go talk to the woman you warned me about." They walked back up to the nurse. "By the way, what's your name?" he asked her. "You brought me a cup of coffee and brought me back to my senses by slapping me in the face, I should at least be able to call you by something besides 'hey nurse'" Again, she shook her head. "Mr. Sloan, you are so right." She looked at Sharise, smiled and said to her, "I really don't like being called 'hey nurse'" she then looked back at Charles, "My name is Judy. And I really prefer that to just about anything else. By the way," she said as she leaned a little closer and in a lower voice, "nobody likes to be called 'hey nurse'." She then stood upright, smiled, and looked over at Sharon. "Mrs. Sloan, you seem to have done a pretty good job with this one." She reached down and pressed a button under the desk, the door behind her opened, "Your wife is in room 4A. And, although I am not supposed to, I will allow your daughter in the room to see her mommy." Sharise's smile disappeared, "She's not my mommy. I don't even like her. She is mean." Judy looked surprised, "I'm sorry, I didn't know." Charles touched her on the shoulder, "Don't worry about it, I didn't know either." He then put his arm around his mother, picked up his little girl and headed to Monica's room leaving Judy standing there more confused than she was when she first met this man. Lloyd followed them into the room, but shortly thereafter, got a phone call and had to leave. As they entered the room, Charles set Sharise down and walked over to the side of the bed. Monica opened her eyes and smiled, "Charles, I am so glad you are here. I am so sorry, no one was supposed to get hurt. Please believe me, I am sorry." Charles bent over, gave her a final kiss on her forehead and softly whispered, "You certainly are." And with that, he took off his wedding ring, placed it on the table next to her, and started out the door, he stopped, looked back at her and said, "By the way, I found my little girl safe and sound, thanks for asking." Monica started sobbing as they left her room. "Charles!! Please Charles! Come back! I'm sorry, I'm so sorry." Charles paused for just a moment, shook his head, and continued down the hall way. Sharon and Sharise were both very happy he had finally come to his senses. Lloyd came running down the hallway, "Charles, Sharon, stop." He yelled. "You need to hear this." Charles was exhausted and didn't want to hear anymore. "Lloyd, if you want to talk to us you need to catch up." They continued through the main door to the waiting room, Charles dad was waiting there. Sharon walked over to him, "Our boy has finally come to his senses. I knew he would. After all, he takes after me." Jack, just shook his head and chuckled.

Lloyd looked over at Jack and nodded. He then turned to Charles. "Charles, I have been trying to tell you. I know who murdered your wife." Charles stopped smiling and the room suddenly got very quiet. "What? What do you mean you know who killed my wife? Why didn't you tell me?" Lloyd rolled his eyes, "I am trying to tell you. That phone call I got?"

"what phone call?" Charles interrupted.

"the one I got as you were walking into Monica's room." Lloyd continued, "and if you would stop interrupting me..."

"yes, Charles, please stop interrupting." Sharon stated, "you know, Lloyd, I tried to teach him better manners, but he takes after his father. He just can't..." Charles grabbed her mouth gently and stopped her from continuing. "Go on Lloyd." He plead. Lloyd continued. "The phone call was from the deputy that took John in. He said he never heard an attorney sing before, but he couldn't get John to shut up. It turns out, Monica had planned to get to know you a long time ago. Apparently, John talked about you a lot. You, Tony, and Jamie." Charles stopped him. "Jamie? Why Jamie?" Lloyd started again, "Charles, do you want to hear this or not?" Charles nodded and sat down. Sharise climbed into his lap. "any way, she knew about you, how much money you were making, and, after John killed her husband, she came up with a plan. she bribed him into finding out where you would be the day she was walking down the beach you and Jamie met at. And, if you believe

John, which I am not sure about yet, she planned everything in order to get ahold of your money and then leave you. She knew that you were too smart to leave it all to her, even if she could get you to marry her. So, she planned the kidnapping. John was supposed to take Sharise and hold onto her until Monica could get away long enough to send a ransom note, knowing you would pay anything to get your 'Angel' back. Then after she got the money, she would sign an affidavit to the fact that her previous husbands death was self-defense, therefore releasing John from any possibility of facing any charges." Lloyd paused. Charles held Sharise a little tighter. "So..." Charles asked, "Who killed my wife, Lloyd? And why?"

"I was just getting to that." Lloyd answered. "According to John; who, by the way, swears he knew nothing about it until this morning, Monica ran Jamie off the road to make sure you were available before she brought the whole idea to John.... Charles, *Monica* murdered Jamie. She tried to take Tony out, because he was interfering with her plans to kidnap Sharise. She thought you would start listening to your friends and family. Since she knew better than to take out another family member, she decided she would remove your friends, one at a time. Since Tony was the one closest to you, she naturally started there. When that failed, she thought she could still salvage her plans by setting up Becky and discrediting him in your eyes. After all, as she said, Tony would do anything to save his wife. What she didn't realize is that Tony would only do anything *within the law* to help his wife. You and I both know that. He would never perjure himself or allow his wife or friends to do so. John thought that if he could get Becky to take the plea bargain they offered her, he would have the insurance he needed to get Monica off his back, and therefore, would not have to go through with the crazy idea of kidnapping anyone's child, especially yours."

Charles couldn't believe it. All this time he had been searching for the person that killed his beloved Jamie and she was living with him as his wife. Pretending to love him just for his money. And, worse, one of his best friends was involved. He couldn't believe it. He also now had to something he really didn't want to do, tell his mother she was right...again.

Printed in the United States
by Bookmasters

Printed in the United States
By Bookmasters